THE NANNY

BOOKS BY DAN GREENBURG

How to Be a Jewish Mother

Kiss My Firm but Pliant Lips

How to Make Yourself Miserable

Chewsday

Jumbo the Boy and Arnold the Elephant

Philly

Porno-Graphics

Scoring

Something's There

Love Kills

What Do Women Want?

How to Avoid Love and Marriage

True Adventures

Confessions of a Pregnant Father

THE NANNY

DAN GREENBURG

MACMILLAN PUBLISHING COMPANY • NEW YORK

COLLIER MACMILLAN PUBLISHERS • LONDON

For Suzanne and Zack

Copyright © 1987 by Dan Greenburg

Macmillan Publishing Company
866 Third Avenue, New York, N.Y. 10022
Collier Macmillan Canada, Inc.

Library of Congress Cataloging-in-Publication Data
Greenburg, Dan.
The nanny.
I. Title.
PS3557.R379N3   1987   813'.54   87-18477
ISBN 0-02-545440-4

Designed by Jack Meserole

Printed in the United States of America

THE NANNY

CHAPTER 1

THE EXCRUCIATING PAIN was gone now. Only the memory of it lingered like the phantom pain of a severed limb. Almost everything human about her had been scourged from her body by the flames. It was actually a relief to be rid of it.

She moved through the deep snow and the thick growth of trees toward the house. She was considerably lighter now—the seventy percent of her body that was water had sizzled, boiled and steamed right out of her in the fire.

She stopped at the last stand of cedar trees. The lights in the house were out. Though her eyes had been burnt out of their sockets, she could see him quite clearly with the part of her that did not require eyes.

What was left of her was pure purpose. Pure purpose and love—overwhelming and uncontrollable love for the man who had done this to her, and a need to be reunited with him and his family that was so great it could forgive him for whatever he had done to her in the past and whatever he might do to her in the future.

Tonight was the worst night of Phil Pressman's life. He was praying it would not be his last.

It was extremely late in the house in the snowy woods of eastern Long Island, possibly as late as 3 a.m., but Phil was afraid to lie down and close his eyes until it got light outside.

The wind was whining through the trees in a particularly unsettling manner. According to the outdoor thermometer, which was swinging back and forth in the wind and knocking against the window as if seeking entrance, the temperature was now hovering slightly above zero.

1

The snapping logs in the fireplace were maintaining the house at a respectable sixty degrees, but the chill that clung to Phil's body had to do with more than temperature. From the floor-to-ceiling windows in the living room Phil could see the foot or two of snow which had fallen onto the ground in the last couple of days and onto the tall cedar trees which engulfed the house.

Now Phil thought he heard a noise at the back door, a soft scratching sound like something trying to get in, and felt his chest tighten and his heart pound and suddenly there didn't seem to be enough air in the room for him to breathe. Please don't let what I think is out there be out there, he prayed.

Something was happening to Phil, his wife and his baby, something hideous, and Phil was still trying to understand what it was and what to do about it and how people as normal and nice as they were could have had such a thing happen to them.

CHAPTER 2

PHIL PRESSMAN AND JULIE STEVENSON grew up in Chicago and met at the U. of I., where Phil was majoring in English with a minor in Psych, and Julie was majoring in Psych with a minor in Art Ed, and if it wasn't love at first sight it was very strong like.

Phil had shaggy brown hair, horn-rimmed glasses, a dry sense of humor and a face that seldom cracked a smile. Julie had platinum hair, a perfect nose, a slim figure and green eyes so nearsighted that even with contacts she squinted. It spoiled her otherwise stunning good looks.

Julie was Catholic, Phil Jewish. Phil's only failing, as far as Julie could see, was that he was an observer in life rather than a participant, a compulsive planner and worrier who found it hard to be in the moment. Julie's only failing, as far as Phil could see, was that she constantly reminded him of this.

After graduation Phil got a job as a copywriter in a small Chicago ad agency and Julie drifted into interior decoration—a cousin of hers worked at the Merchandise Mart and tossed her occasional jobs she deemed too small or boring to do herself.

Though Julie wished audibly to be married, she and Phil lived together in sin for four years. One day Phil, who was not given to impulsive gestures, announced:

"I've got a great idea."

"*I'll* be the judge of that," said Julie.

"What do you say we take a cab down to City Hall, wearing our jeans and sneakers, and get married?"

"Perfect," said Julie.

Julie had yearned for a big romantic wedding with a white gown and yards of lace, but wanted to be supportive of Phil's rare attempts at spontaneity. Also she knew Phil was too nervous about the commitment of marriage to make a big deal out of a wedding. So she let fear of commitment masquerade as coolness and pretended that the impulsive jeans-and-sneakers job at City Hall was her kind of thing.

Before they knew it Phil and Julie were thirty years old.

"I think it's time we got serious about our careers," said Phil, "and move to New York."

"I think it's time we got serious about starting a family," said Julie, "and move to a larger apartment."

"Starting a family should wait till our careers are further along," said Phil.

"In case you didn't recognize that ticking sound you hear," said Julie, "it's my biological clock."

Phil sent out feelers to the top ten ad agencies in New York. One was a medium-sized shop by the name of Sullivan, Stouffer,

3

Cohn and McConnell, which had been making a name for itself with Babe, the light beer for women. They flew him to Manhattan for an interview with their president, a colorful sixty-five-year-old woman named Mary Margaret Sullivan.

Phil was surprised at Sullivan's beauty. Her hair was steel, her eyelashes long and dark, her skin inexplicably tan. She was of medium height and still had quite a trim figure.

She studied Phil's portfolio with great interest. There was an ad for an overnight depilatory which promised a "no-wax shine," headlined "Hair Today, Gone Tomorrow." There was an ad for a candy company which showed a child putting a chocolate lollipop into his mouth, headlined "So long, sucker." There was an ad for a lipstick, headlined "Kiss me, you fool."

On his sample reel was a commercial for a paper towel called Sponge-on-a-Roll. The commercial showed a length of towel sucking up a huge spill, and the soundtrack featured the exaggerated noise of water going down a bathtub drain. The only copy, in a cartoon balloon above the spill, was the word "Slurp!"

"Your work is clever," said Sullivan.

"Thank you," said Phil.

"That isn't necessarily a compliment," said Sullivan. "Clever advertising is usually clever at the expense of a strong sales message."

"The ads I've seen of *yours*," said Phil, "have a strong sales message and they're also clever."

"Good reply," she said. "Tell me, why do you think I ought to hire you?"

Phil thought this over a moment.

"Because I'm really good, but there's a lot that you can still teach me," he said.

She laughed.

"All right," she said.

Sullivan's offer was frankly less than Phil had heard he was worth in New York. But he liked the idea of working for her, it was his only firm offer, and besides she *had* flown him out there. Phil accepted the job.

That February, a brutal month in Chicago when the wind off Lake Michigan was so strong it could literally knock you over, Phil and Julie Pressman moved to New York.

CHAPTER 3

FEBRUARY in New York was cold and dead but not like Chicago. There was no hard shell of pitted gray ice on the streets all winter long. There were no weeks of temperatures with windchill-factor readings in the range of liquid nitrogen.

"Compared to Chicago," Phil observed happily, "New York is goddam Fort Lauderdale."

They arrived in the middle of a garbage strike. Mountains of refuse tied up in Hefty trash bags lined the streets like levees on a rising river. They looked at thirty-nine apartments in the first week.

"I thought the rents were high in *Chicago*," Julie exclaimed. "I can't *believe* the rents in New York."

Julie found a place on the Lower West Side in the wholesale meat district. The neighborhood was lively and fascinating, its narrow cobbled streets crowded with unloading tractor-trailer rigs and stocky men in blood-splattered white coats hauling huge wet slabs of meat around on their shoulders.

The apartment on Perry Street was in a building that had once been a pickle factory. Julie thought one of the two smaller bedrooms would be fine for a baby, even though Phil had made her agree to wait a year before getting pregnant. The other little bedroom, which Phil thought he could use as a mini-office, had a partial view of the Hudson River if you stood on a chair. The master bedroom had quite a good view of a brick wall across an airshaft with the stenciled message, "Generic Graffito."

The wholesale meat district was not one of the more desirable neighborhoods in Manhattan, but it was dearer than they'd thought. Every time they'd seen the apartment was in the morning when the area was crawling with trucks and men in white coats hauling sides of meat. When they moved in they discovered that meat-related activities began about 3 a.m. and ended at noon. After lunch the warehouses and loading docks shut down for the day, the trucks were parked and the meat workers went home.

By night the area was abandoned and ominous, all dark warehouses, empty loading docks, driverless diesel rigs. Men in black leather, chains and sunglasses lurked in doorways, and a different sort of meat market prevailed.

"Oh, great." Phil groaned. "We're living in the heart of New York's sado-masochist gay community."

Julie soon found the equivalent of the patronizing cousin in Chicago who gave her decorating jobs too small or boring to do herself.

Phil was given three accounts to work on at the agency: a non-dairy ice cream substitute made from soybeans called Lite-'N'-Kreemy, an antiperspirant called No Sweat and a men's hair spray from the same company called Hold It. Not a heroic trio of products, but all three were packaged goods with major media buys in TV, so the agency was receiving commissions big enough to value the people who worked on the accounts.

Shortly after moving into their new apartment, Julie conceived. Though it had been an accident, she was pleased. Phil was apprehensive.

"It's not the right time for us to be having a baby," he said.

"Why not?" said Julie.

6

"We've just moved here," said Phil. "I've just started a new job. I may be making enough to support two of us, but not three. We can't afford it now."

"What about what *I* make?" said Julie, hurt that Phil never took her income seriously.

"Even *with* what you make," said Phil, "we can't afford it now."

"I think money is a false issue," said Julie, who was good at spotting false issues, having been a Psych major.

"What do you mean?" said Phil.

"I think you're afraid of the commitment of parenthood, and you're just focusing on the money because it's an easier issue."

"I'm not going to deny that I'm apprehensive about the commitment of parenthood," said Phil. "But a big part of my apprehension really *is* the expense."

"Come on, Phil."

"Come on yourself. Did you know it now costs a million dollars to put a kid through school in New York?"

"Where did you get that figure?" said Julie.

"It doesn't *matter* where I got it," said Phil. "That's what it costs for a decent education in New York, what with private schools and all—you *have* to send your kid to private school in New York unless you want to have him mugged and raped every day. And then there are the other expenses: food, clothes, toys, doctor bills, nannies . . . I suppose you'd expect the kid to have a nanny, too?"

"We'd need somebody to take care of the baby when we're not here, wouldn't we?"

"Well, we can't afford a nanny," said Phil. "Plus which, we're both very private people. I can't see us living with a complete stranger in our home, can you?"

"Somehow this discussion has stopped being about whether or not we're having a baby and started being about whether or not we're having a *nanny*," said Julie.

Phil heaved a tremendous sigh. Julie looked at him a moment, then took both of his hands in hers.

7

"Phil, we did agree I'd get pregnant in a year," she said, "and we did rent an apartment big enough for a baby, didn't we?"

"So?"

"So I'm pregnant now. I don't know how it happened, because I really did think it was safe. What do you want me to do, have an abortion?"

Phil sighed again and shook his head.

"No, of course not."

"Then why don't we just both enter into the joyousness of the pregnancy and try to be in the moment, and not be so apprehensive? Why don't we say yes to life? Having a baby is an *adventure*, Phil, a wonderful *adventure*, especially if you're a participant and not an observer. If you don't want to have a nanny, then O.K., we'll both work out some way of doing part of our work at home and maybe we *can* take care of the baby ourselves."

Phil thought it over and then took his wife in his arms and kissed her. He was starting to get very turned on at the thought of what they'd created by making love. He wanted very much to go to bed then and there, but Julie said she wasn't really into it at the moment, and so they didn't.

CHAPTER 4

THE PREGNANCY progressed without complications. The weather turned mild. Dead trees budded and exploded into bloom. Julie's bosom and belly, initially slow to swell, now filled like balloons fitted over water faucets.

Julie stood naked in front of the bathroom mirror and admired her breasts from various angles.

"Just look at these things, Phil," she said proudly. "I've gone from 34C to 36DD and they're still growing. I've outgrown six bras."

"Why don't you call up Dolly Parton and see whether she has any old ones she could lend you?"

"Dolly Parton's bras wouldn't fit me anymore," said Julie. "These are the breasts that ate Pittsburgh."

They began Lamaze classes. They bought a bassinet, a Snugli for carrying the baby on their chests, a collapsible carry-bed, a collapsible stroller, dozens of plastic baby bottles, nipples and pacifiers. They bought tiny T-shirts and tiny Nike tennis shoes and tiny pajamas with bunnies on them.

Phil worried that buying so much before the baby came might be a jinx. Julie tried to kid him out of it. An account exec at Phil's agency told him about an old Jewish superstition of tying red ribbons around the purchases to ward off evil. Phil bought and tied red ribbons.

Both Phil and Julie worried how the pregnancy would affect their sex life. Phil told Julie he found her rapidly inflating breasts and belly more turn-on than turn-off, but they didn't manage to make love more than once every couple of weeks.

They both came up with endless excuses for not having sex. One of them usually took so long in the bathroom getting ready for bed that the other became angry or fell asleep. During the steamy summer months they rationalized it was too hot for sex, but in the fall the frequency of their lovemaking didn't accelerate.

On those rare occasions when they did have satisfying sex, they were irritable the next day and often had senseless marital squabbles. Julie said the things they fought about were false issues. She said their intimacy was threatening to Phil. Phil said she still sounded like a Psych major.

Though increasingly horny, Phil claimed he was nervous about crushing the fetus during intercourse. Both felt self-conscious about having sex with a child present. Julie said she might be able to overcome her self-consciousness with wine, but although the obstetrician had said a glass every now and again couldn't hurt, Phil was terrified of birth defects and wouldn't let her have it. As a result, they continued to have sex infrequently, and when they did Phil often couldn't stay hard long enough for Julie to come.

Then it was November, Julie's ninth month. The snow began to fall in short, tentative flurries. The obstetrician informed them Julie was dilated two centimeters—sex was canceled till sometime in mid-January, six weeks after delivery. This news was received by both with a mixture of frustration and relief.

Julie's water broke during Thanksgiving dinner. In the admissions room of New York Hospital an intern warned them to protect their valuables:

"We've had three expectant mothers mugged in labor rooms on the maternity floor in the past two weeks," he confided, "and a woman who was coming out of general anesthesia in the recovery room found a thief pulling her wedding ring off her finger."

"Jesus," said Julie, "having a baby in New York Hospital is as safe as having one on the goddam subway."

They wheeled her to a tiny labor room on the maternity floor, and for the first few hours everything went according to plan. Phil and Julie practiced their Lamaze breathing and it seemed to help. But by the time Julie had dilated five centimeters the pain was unbearable.

"Phil, I changed my mind." Julie sobbed. "I don't want a baby after all—get me out of here!"

Phil tried to comfort her, but felt frightened and powerless to deal with her agony. The delivery itself was bloody and terrifying. Nothing in Lamaze classes had prepared either of them for the pain—nothing in the classroom films of smiling women delivering effortlessly, their babies sliding out of their vaginas like greased piglets.

In the final hour Phil became convinced that both Julie and the baby were going to die on the delivery table. He began silent negotiations with the Deity in which he gave up success in his career in exchange for the lives of his wife and child.

Julie's screams caused nurses to appear at the delivery room door and warn that she was scaring all the other women on the floor. Julie apologized, but continued to scream.

The baby, a boy, emerged unscathed.

CHAPTER 5

WHEN THE NIGHT NURSE entered the man's room, at first she thought he was asleep. Then she realized his eyes were open.

"Good evening, Mr. Parsons," she said.

"Good evening," he said.

"I thought you were asleep," she said.

"No," he said, "I wasn't."

"Would you like to go to sleep now?" she said.

"Not particularly," he said.

"Would you like to watch TV?"

"Not particularly," he said.

"Would you like to read?"

"Not particularly," he said.

"Would you like me to turn on the lights?"

"Not particularly," he said.

"Would you like a snack?"

"Not particularly," he said.

"Then what can I do for you?" she said.

"Not a thing," he said. "I'm quite content."

"Really?" she said.

"Really," he said. "Quite content."

"You don't *seem* content," she said. "You seem extremely depressed."

"How odd," said the man. "I have never been happier in my life."

CHAPTER 6

PHIL AND JULIE brought the tiny newborn home from the hospital. Phil was awkward handling the baby at first, afraid he'd injure him.

The baby's fingers and hands were in constant motion, like sea anemones underwater. Phil gazed at his new son in awe, marveled at his unusually thick brown hair and intelligent blue eyes, marveled at the microscopic fingers and toes. Phil felt chest-swelling pride in his child's creation, yet marginal responsibility for its detailing, felt fierce protectiveness of his child's health, yet poignant ignorance of its maintenance.

For Phil the concept of actually being anyone's father, when he was scarcely sure he could take care of *himself*, was one he'd have to grow into.

Their friends in Chicago who had children urged them to hire a baby nurse for at least a few weeks, but they'd decided to care for the baby themselves and didn't want to dilute the achievement with temporary help. Julie's folks flew in to help make the first few days less difficult. Phil and Julie were grateful, at least in the beginning, and put them up in the tiny room next to the baby's.

Julie, who was determined to breast-feed, didn't start producing milk for the first few days. Her breasts appeared twice their normal size, but when the baby sucked on them all he got out was a colorless liquid called colostrum. Phil felt that Julie's breasts, once his to fondle and enjoy, were now exclusively the baby's turf, and this erected a subtle barrier between him and them.

"When *I* was nursing *Julie*," reminisced Mrs. Stevenson, "I had so much milk I leaked all over the sheets."

"I don't *have* any milk—how can I be a good mother?" said Julie, and began to weep.

"Don't worry, your milk is going to kick in any day now," said Phil.

Phil hoped Julie's weeping was merely postpartum depression, but the thick-haired baby cried incessantly and both Julie's mom and dad worried aloud.

"The poor thing is going to die of malnutrition," said her father.

"That's utter nonsense," said Phil, but he secretly feared the man was right.

Julie's mother watched the baby nurse at Julie's empty breast. "There's nothing there, is there, precious?" cooed her mother to the baby. "You're sucking death."

Phil's jaw dropped, but Julie's mom explained that sucking death was a regional expression from her girlhood and was not meant literally.

When Phil tried to give the baby a bath in the sink, Julie's mom and dad supervised his technique, couching their mounting anxiety in the form of studiedly diplomatic rhetorical questions:

"Philip," said Julie's father, "don't you think that water's a little too hot for him?"

"Philip," said Julie's mother, "don't you think that sink is a little too full?"

"You don't think you're getting soap in his eyes, do you?" said Julie's mother.

"Wouldn't you say he's too near the edge of the sink?" said Julie's father.

They made Phil so frantic he nearly dropped the baby on the floor. Julie's folks flew back to Chicago and Phil and Julie were relieved to be alone with their son. Phil took a two-week paternity leave from the agency without pay.

They'd named the baby Harry. He was both more beautiful and more vulnerable-looking than they'd expected. He studied Phil with such an intelligent expression that Phil was sure he was memorizing every feature of his face. They kept Harry in a white wicker bassinet in their bedroom and they were seldom able to sleep more than three hours a night. It was murder.

"I can't take this," said Phil one day, staggering painfully about the apartment. "Every muscle in my body is screaming from lack of sleep."

"*You* can't take it?" said Julie. "*You're* not the one who's getting up to nurse him every hour and a half."

"I'm beginning to understand why they use sleep deprivation to torture prisoners of war," said Phil.

By the start of the second week things had improved a little. Harry was still alive. He had not perished from parental ignorance. Julie's breasts began producing an uneven flow of milk and Harry seemed less cranky.

The sight of Julie cradling the baby in her arms and nursing him, and their obvious mutual pleasure, reassured Phil that they had done a marvelous thing. Julie adored Harry. Harry clearly adored Julie.

They were beginning to get more confident about the processes of changing his diapers, burping him, bathing him and handling him. They were less afraid of dropping him or inadvertently snapping off his impossibly tiny fingers while dressing or undressing him.

By the middle of the second week, although Julie's milk was still not flowing freely, Harry appeared to be getting enough to survive, and they started to think they'd be able to cope after all.

But at the end of the second week, when Phil was ending his paternity leave, Harry began crying again, this time uncontrollably, sometimes for two or three hours without stopping. The crying was desperate in tone, the sound of a creature in agony. He grimaced in pain and drew his tiny knees up to his chest and shrieked. It was as if he were mirroring the excruciating pain of his own delivery.

They took him to a pediatrician, who couldn't find anything wrong. The grandparents phoned frequently with advice:

"Don't you think you ought to pick him up whenever he cries?" said Julie's diplomatic mother. "Just to reassure him?"

"*Never* pick him up when he cries," said Phil's undiplomatic mother. "It will spoil him rotten."

"Have you tried feeding him fennel tea in his bottle?" said Julie's mother. "Just to soothe his stomach?"

"Put him on top of the washing machine in the spin cycle," said Phil's mother. "It will distract him."

"Walk him around the room and bounce him," said Phil's father. "It will get rid of the gas."

They tried to follow everyone's advice. Bouncing was the only thing that worked consistently.

Phil's folks flew in for a few days to help, and Phil returned to the agency. As with Julie's parents, at first their presence was appreciated, then it produced more problems than it solved. Phil's parents had the same fears about their son's and daughter-in-law's competence to handle a newborn but didn't couch them diplomatically.

"These diaper wipes are no good," said Phil's mom. "They'll dry out his skin. Don't change him too near the edge of the changing table. And don't pick him up every time he cries or you'll encourage him to cry. And don't walk around the house whispering whenever he sleeps or he'll never learn to sleep with normal room noise."

Phil's folks flew back to Chicago, and Phil went in to see Mary Margaret Sullivan to request another leave of absence.

CHAPTER 7

MARY MARGARET SULLIVAN was, at sixty-five, something of a legend in the advertising business.

She wrote witty, soft-sell ads for Cushman shock absorbers and created Cushman Shock Therapy Clinics all across the country. She wrote witty, soft-sell ads for a British diaper called Nappies and created a toll-free Nappy Hotline which nervous parents could call at any hour of the day or night and talk to a registered nurse about infant problems.

At first she was very particular about whom she selected as clients. She accepted no tobacco or liquor clients. She accepted only clients whose products were the best in their respective areas of the marketplace.

But the commissions from these quality products were not enough and she was soon forced to make compromises. She accepted a dishwashing detergent called Sparkle Plenty that sometimes left streaks. She picked up a men's cologne called Fatal Attraction from a company rumored to have part of its money laundered in the Cayman Islands.

Although she still balked at liquor clients, she took on a light beer account. Despairing of being able to differentiate it from its competitors, she convinced the client to position it as the first *women's* beer. She devised a commercial in which several attractive but raucous young women hassle a male stripper in a private strip club, and saw the spot make Babe an instantaneous hit.

When Phil was ushered into Sullivan's office he thought she seemed distracted.

"How's the new baby, Pressman?" she said, rising to shake his hand.

"Not great," said Phil. "He cries all the time."

"That's what babies do," she said, "cry."

16

"I mean all the time," he said. "The doctors don't know what it is."

"It's colic," said Sullivan.

"Oh, I hope not."

"That's what it is," she said.

Phil didn't want to argue with her.

"In any case," he said, "I'm afraid I'm going to have to take another leave of absence, because Julie can't take care of him by herself."

"Don't you have a nurse?" she said.

"No, we wanted to take care of him ourselves."

"That's nonsense. The child has colic. Get a nurse."

"Well, maybe we will, but I really have to take another leave of absence, because—"

"Don't take a leave of absence, work at home a lot."

"You wouldn't mind?" said Phil.

"Why should I mind?" she said. "*I* do it."

"Well, thanks," he said, "thanks very much."

She extended her hand, signifying that the meeting was over. He shook it and went to the door.

"And for God's sake, Pressman," she said, "get a nurse."

CHAPTER 8

CHRISTMAS AND CHANUKKAH were coming. Phil and Julie had been so busy with the baby they hadn't had time to send cards or buy presents. They figured they might get around to it by February and hoped friends and family would understand.

17

The baby continued his ceaseless crying. Phil and Julie took him back to the pediatrician, who said it sounded like colic. They'd heard the horror stories about colic and refused to believe their baby had it.

"He *can't* have colic," said Julie. "For the first two weeks his crying wasn't even all that bad."

"That's when colic tends to show up," said the pediatrician, "after the first two weeks."

"How long does it last?" said Phil, recalling Mary Margaret Sullivan's certainty of what it was.

"About three months," said the doctor.

"Three *months?*" said Phil. "You mean he's going to be crying for three months, for three hours at a stretch?"

"No," said the doctor, "colicky babies cry up to *ten* hours at a stretch."

Phil and Julie were momentarily speechless.

"How do you treat colic?" said Julie finally.

"You don't," said the doctor.

"What?"

"Nobody knows what colic is," said the doctor. "There isn't any cure."

When they left the doctor's office, Julie proposed a number of ideas, chief among which was slashing her wrists. They realized they would have to hire someone to help with the baby after all.

Phil took out the Yellow Pages and called every employment agency in the book which placed domestics. The agencies were not encouraging. Phil and Julie were not offering enough money to attract good people, they said. The holiday season was not the right time to get good people, they said.

A lack of good people did not deter the agencies from sending Phil and Julie grazing herds of applicants. A sorry procession of would-be nannies, the majority of whom had no experience with babies of any age, most of whom were incapable of carrying on the humblest conversation in English, shuffled through their living room.

They took pity on these women and tried to spend at least ten minutes with each one, even when it was instantly obvious the person they were interviewing was tragically unqualified for the job. They knew it was a waste of precious time, but they were too kind to reject somebody after meeting her for only a couple of minutes.

They were becoming resigned to the idea that they would never find anyone responsible or confident enough to handle a colicky baby, when one of the agencies told them about a nanny who had just become available—an experienced British woman named Luci Redman who, before becoming a nanny, had been a nurse.

She sounded ideal. They wondered if they'd be able to afford someone that well-qualified, but with visions of Mary Poppins dancing in their heads, they made an appointment to see Luci Redman the following day.

CHAPTER 9

LUCI REDMAN was astonishing looking.

She had high cheekbones and long straight hair so black it was almost blue, and blue eyes so light in color and so piercing it wasn't pleasant to look directly into them. You might have described her face as beautiful, except there was something severe and off-putting about it.

Perhaps it was that she wore no makeup. Perhaps it was her skin, which looked much older than the rest of her. She appeared to be in her mid-thirties, but her skin looked closer to mid-fifties. She was big-boned and solidly built. She stood at least six feet tall.

When they'd gotten past her imposing appearance, Phil and Julie noticed her manner. It was patronizing. It was mildly disrespectful. It was as if *they* were being interviewed, not she.

She asked them three questions to every one of theirs: "What have you done to educate yourselves about becoming parents? What schedule do you currently follow and how do you expect it to change? What is your knowledge of nutrition? What are your views on discipline? What made you decide to become parents? Was the baby planned?"

Phil and Julie exchanged bemused looks. They decided against hiring her. Then the baby awakened and began his frenzied crying. Luci Redman strode to Harry's bassinet and, without so much as seeking permission to do so, picked him up. The baby whimpered a moment and then stopped crying. Phil and Julie were impressed in spite of themselves.

As long as Luci Redman held Harry he looked content. The moment she put him down he resumed his torturous crying.

"You seem to have a way with babies," said Julie.

Luci Redman reacted as though this were a statement so obvious as to be banal.

"It's just a matter of knowing how to hold them," she said.

Phil and Julie exchanged looks.

"Might I see the nanny's quarters?" said Luci Redman.

"Oh, of course," said Julie, leading the way to the small bedroom next to the baby's.

Luci Redman gave it scarcely a glance.

"Have you nothing larger?" she inquired, as if she were inspecting hotel accommodations.

Phil rolled his eyes, but Julie was apologetic. She explained they'd wanted to get a larger apartment but couldn't afford one. Phil glared at his wife, appalled she was making excuses for their apartment and pleading poverty to a total stranger.

Although they hadn't asked, Luci Redman informed them what she required as salary, and it was substantially less than what they'd feared. Phil was still about to say they were considering several other applicants when Luci Redman advised them she would consider their position and let them know in about a week.

Phil and Julie again exchanged looks—the nanny would let *them* know, right?

Luci Redman put on her long black hooded overcoat and walked to the door. The baby began to cry again. Luci Redman strode back into the room, plucked him out of Julie's arms, and once more Harry whimpered slightly and became silent.

Luci Redman left them several xeroxed letters of recommendation and then she was gone. Julie turned to Phil with a questioning expression.

"I don't like her," said Phil. "She's creepy."

"Jesus, I don't like her either," said Julie, "but you have to admit she's great with the baby."

"She's great with the baby," said Phil, "but I'm not willing to put up with what I'd have to put up with if I hired her. Tell the truth, would *you* be willing to live with what you just saw?"

Julie looked at Phil, inhaled slowly, held her breath a moment and pursed her lips. Phil waited. At length, Julie closed her eyes, exhaled audibly and shook her head.

"I guess not," said Julie. "But she sure would have been great with the baby."

CHAPTER 10

JUST OUT OF CURIOSITY they skimmed Luci Redman's letters of recommendation. One was from a dermatologist in Palm Beach, Florida, one from an investment banker in Detroit, Michigan, one from the president of a small oil company in Houston, Texas. All three were absolutely adulatory.

"*These* people didn't seem to have too much trouble putting up with her," said Julie.

"Some people like domineering household help," said Phil.

"I know," said Julie. "It reminds them of their parents."

They put Luci Redman's letters in a desk drawer.

One night shortly before Christmas, fearing they'd have no holiday at all unless he did something about it, Phil went to an abandoned pier on the Hudson River where they were selling Christmas trees. He surveyed the sorry assortment of scrawny unbought firs.

Humming a favorite Christmas carol from the Dolly Parton–Kenny Rogers album and wondering whether he was compromising millions of Jews throughout history who had died rather than give up their religion, Phil tried to strike a bargain for the least worst tree, a Scotch pine with one grotesquely barren side.

The Hispanic gentleman in the black leather motorcycle jacket and sunglasses who sold it to him was unwilling to lower his price upon learning of the tree's deformity, and was not impressed to hear that even a *healthy* Scotch pine of this size would have been a third the price in Chicago.

Phil paid the asking price, dragged the tree back to the apartment and erected it in the living-dining room, being careful to hide the bad side against the wall. The tree got only minimally decorated, however, because during this period Harry was crying for five, six, even seven hours at a stretch.

They paced miles with Harry each night. They telephoned other pediatricians and asked their advice. All claimed that there was no cure for colic. All claimed that no one knew what colic was. One doctor decreed that colic didn't exist.

Harry's crying took on an angry, savage quality. Combined with their average sleep of three hours per night, his crying was pushing both Phil and Julie to the edge. Each wondered why they'd had a baby to begin with, why they'd gotten married, why they'd had the misfortune of being born.

Their love for the baby was, at this point, reflexive and theoretical. It was hard for either of them to look at the red-faced, squalling infant and feel deep affection. It was easier to look at him and consider that he had irrevocably ruined their once-pleasant lives.

Phil and Julie snapped at each other, then apologized, then snapped again. They barely talked to their parents on the phone. Between communications vital to baby care they gave each other the silent treatment.

On the first night of Chanukkah Phil realized they had no menorah. All the stores he went to were out of both menorahs and Chanukkah candles. As a compromise Phil bought birthday candles, stuck them into a stale cupcake, lit them and said the blessings. Birthday candles on a stale cupcake. Phil felt he had let down the whole religion.

On Christmas Eve Phil and Julie exchanged no presents and a total of seventeen words. After the baby finally went to sleep, they ate frozen Manhandler turkey dinners and watched a TV rebroadcast of *Midnight Mass at the Vatican*.

It was somehow not the image either Phil or Julie had had of Christmas or Chanukkah or marriage or parenthood. Each felt overwhelmed, trapped and hopeless. Each tried to recall his life before the baby. Each envied anyone who was still single.

During the week following Christmas they somehow managed to interview nineteen more applicants for the nanny job, including two elderly ladies and three girls in their late teens, all of whom were breathtakingly incompetent, and a handicapped woman who arrived in a fat-tired electric wheelchair.

The only positive value in being interviewers was that they found themselves uniting against the interviewees.

CHAPTER 11

EARLY IN THE EVENING of December 31, when the last job seeker had departed, Julie and Phil slumped into chairs in the living room.

"I can't do this anymore, Phil," said Julie, beginning to weep. "I really can't. I'm losing it."

Phil reached over and tried to comfort her.

"It'll get better, babe," he said without conviction. "I promise."

The telephone rang.

"It'll *have* to get better, Phil," said Julie, sobbing, "because if it doesn't I'm really going to have a breakdown. I may be having one anyway."

Phil did not appreciate talk of breakdowns. He saw them as distinct possibilities. The phone rang again. Sighing, Phil got up and answered it. Julie sobbed quietly in the background.

"Yeah," said Phil gruffly.

"Mr. Pressman," said the unmistakable British voice, "this is Miss Redman."

Phil's eyebrows went up.

"Yes, Miss Redman," said Phil.

Julie stopped sobbing to listen.

"I have considered your position, Mr. Pressman, and find that, on the whole, I am inclined to accept it after all."

"I see," said Phil.

"If you still want me, of course."

If you still *want* me? The uncharacteristic flash of vulnerability impressed him.

"Could you hold the wire a moment, please, Miss Redman?"

"Certainly."

Phil covered the mouthpiece with his palm and leaned in Julie's direction.

"Luci Redman has considered our position and finds that, on the whole, she is inclined to accept it after all," he said sotto voce. "If we still *want* her, of course."

"If we still *want* her?" said Julie, eyebrows on the rise. "She actually used those words?"

"As God is my witness," said Phil.

Julie's eyebrows crept higher. Phil waited, his palm still covering the mouthpiece of the telephone.

"Well?" said Phil.

"Well *what?*" said Julie. "Jesus, don't tell me you'd actually *hire* her?"

"My God, Julie, what are my choices?" said Phil. "I can either hire Luci Redman or I can pack you off to the rubber room."

Julie smiled and touched Phil's arm.

"I suppose we ought to call a few of her references," said Julie.

"I suppose we ought to," said Phil. "Although they'll probably just repeat on the phone what they said in the letters."

"You're probably right," said Julie.

"Do you want me to tell her to wait a few days while we check her out, or do you think that'll make us lose her?"

Julie sighed.

"I think waiting that long might make us lose *me*," said Julie. Silence.

"So?" said Phil. "What should I tell her?"

Julie looked at Phil.

"Can we afford her?" she said.

"Not really. Next question."

Julie thought a moment.

"What would *you* tell her?" she said.

"I'd tell her to get over here as fast as her hot little legs will carry her," said Phil.

Julie smiled for the first time in a week.

"O.K. then," she said. "Go ahead and hire her."

Phil got back on the phone.

"Miss Redman?"

"Yes, Mr. Pressman?"

"How soon would you be able to start?"

A slight pause.

"Would tomorrow morning be agreeable?"

"*Tomorrow?*" said Phil. "You mean New Year's Day?"

There was a brief pause.

"Yes, if that is convenient for you."

Phil flashed a look at Julie. She shrugged.

"Tomorrow morning would be *splendid*, Miss Redman."

When Phil hung up the receiver, Julie buried her face in his neck.

"Happy New Year, baby," she said, her tears now those of joy.

"Happy New Year, sweetheart," said Phil. "God, what a wonderful way to start the new year!"

"Everything is going to be all right now," said Julie, "isn't it?"

"Everything is going to be perfect now," said Phil.

"I love you, Phil," she said and kissed him.

"I love you, too," he said and kissed her, hugging her close and feeling his eyes begin to water.

A pause.

"Phil?"

"Mmmm?"

"What did you mean by 'hot little legs'?"

CHAPTER 12

THE FOLLOWING MORNING, New Year's Day, at seven sharp, Luci Redman arrived and moved into Phil and Julie Pressman's apartment.

26

If it had been a normal New Year's Day, thought Julie, Luci Redman would have found them hung over and asleep. On this particular New Year's Day they were stone sober and had already been up for two hours.

Luci Redman had brought with her only two pieces of luggage. Julie noted that they were severely scuffed calfskin, but obviously expensive. By 7:35 Luci Redman had unpacked and organized her room, changed into a starched white nurse's uniform, changed the baby and given him his bath in the little bathroom between the nanny's and baby's bedrooms.

Julie watched the bath with great interest. The way that Luci Redman was bathing Harry was not the way they'd been taught to bathe him at the class on bathing at the hospital. Julie was at first reluctant to mention this, for fear of hurting the woman's feelings. And then she figured, what the hell, she *works* for us.

"That's not how they taught us to bathe him in the class on bathing at the hospital," Julie said.

"Perhaps not," said Luci Redman. "But that is how we shall bathe him from now on, dear."

Julie felt stupid.

By 8:20 Luci Redman had reorganized all the baby's paraphernalia in the kitchen and redone the changing table in the bedroom which they'd prepared for him but not yet used, and she had also observed Julie breast-feeding and informed her that she was holding him wrong.

"But that's the way they taught us to hold him in breast-feeding class," said Julie.

"Perhaps so," said Luci Redman pleasantly. "But now we shall do it the *right* way, dear."

Julie supposed Luci Redman was right, but she really resented being criticized.

By 9:15 Luci Redman had reorganized all the rest of the things in the kitchen and made Julie and Phil a large English breakfast. Julie was awed by the woman's energy and tried to overcome her own wounded pride with a gesture of friendliness.

27

"Why don't you join us?" said Julie, smiling.

Luci Redman looked nonplussed for a moment.

"In my country, Mrs. Pressman," said Luci Redman, "servants do not dine with their employers."

Julie's cheeks and forehead got very flushed. It serves me right, thought Julie, it really serves me goddam right for trying to be friendly.

"Well, Luci," said Julie, "we're not quite so formal in this country."

"Begging your pardon, Mrs. Pressman, but *I* am," said Luci Redman.

"Very well then, Luci," said Julie carefully, "we will respect your wishes."

"Also, Mrs. Pressman, I prefer not to be called Luci, if you don't mind."

Julie closed her eyes. Luci Redman is a damned difficult woman, she thought to herself, but she is industrious, energetic and experienced, and if I can just stay out of her way she might save our marriage and my sanity.

"What would you prefer to be called?" said Julie.

"Nanny," said Nanny.

"Fine," said Julie. "Then Nanny it is."

"Thank you," said Nanny. "And now, since you both look frightful from lack of sleep, I suggest you lie down for a nap while I dispense with the dishes."

There was clearly no arguing with the woman. Julie exchanged covert looks with Phil, who appeared to be somewhat amused by Nanny. Well, thought Julie, some people are frequently amused by hubris, at least initially.

In their bedroom Phil and Julie whispered and giggled about Nanny like naughty children, and Julie did a deft parody of her, accent and all.

"In *my* country, Mrs. Pressman," said Julie in an exaggeratedly prissy upper-class British accent, mincing haughtily about the bedroom, "servants do not *dine* with their em-*ploy*-ers."

They both giggled some more, but then they lay down and relaxed for the first time since they'd brought the baby home four weeks ago.

Nanny might be overbearing and opinionated, thought Julie, but it was clear that she had things very well in hand.

CHAPTER 13

THE TWO NURSES stood outside Mr. Parsons's room.

"I don't know what to do with him," said the younger nurse. "He just lies there and looks at the ceiling, all day and all night. And when I ask him if he wants to go to sleep or watch TV or read or have something to eat or have the light on or have the light off, all he'll say is 'Not particularly.' And when I ask him what I can do for him, he says nothing, everything is perfect, he's never been happier in his life. I really don't know what to do with him."

"Mr. Parsons has suffered a terrible tragedy," said the older nurse. "Right now, just lying and looking at the ceiling is all he is willing to do. Right now he is doing the best that he can."

"But this has been going on for weeks," said the younger nurse. "Isn't he ever going to want to do anything but lie there and stare at the ceiling?"

"If you had been through what Mr. Parsons has been through," said the older nurse, "lying in bed and looking at the ceiling might be all you'd want to do, too."

CHAPTER 14

ALTHOUGH Harry ceased crying every time Nanny picked him up, Nanny pronounced it bad training to pick him up every time he cried, and so he still wailed for lengthy periods. The sound was like dripping acid on his parents' nerves.

Phil returned to the agency and looked for further excuses to be out of the apartment.

Between breast-feedings, Julie helped Nanny with Harry and tried to get back into the decorating business.

Phil wrote a commercial for No Sweat antiperspirant which featured a crew of sweating, bare-chested sailors in the boiler room of a ship working alongside a dapper gent in a white dinner jacket. It looked to be 130 degrees in the boiler room, but the dapper gent was bone dry. Although everybody at the agency, from Sullivan on down, loved the spot, the client hated it, and Phil was spirited silently off the account.

At about the same time, the Lite-'N'-Kreemy folks found their sales slipping and shortly thereafter the account left the agency for Wells Rich Greene.

In place of Lite-'N'-Kreemy and No Sweat, Phil was assigned a glass spray called On A Clear Day and an instant coffee so new it didn't yet have a name. Phil was invited, along with most of the creative staff, to submit names for the new product.

Phil's boss on both the new accounts was a gruff-voiced, Brillo-haired account executive named Ralph Roberts. Phil's first meeting with Roberts took place in the account exec's office along with the art director assigned to both products, a young Italian-American named Tony Davinci.

Phil hadn't yet worked with the handsome, trendily dressed art director, but he liked Tony's irreverent attitude toward the agency, an attitude not much admired in the industry since the early 1960s.

"Gentlemen," said Roberts, "I thank you for the product names you submitted to me. I thought some of them were amusing, but I'm not going to propose Not The Same Old Grind or I Can't Believe It Has No Caffeine to the client. Consolidated Foods isn't long on humor."

"What are the front-runners?" said Tony.

"Morning Roast and Mountain Aroma," said Roberts.

Tony whistled in mock appreciation.

"Morning Roast," he said. "Beautiful. It sounds like you're giving them a slice of beef for breakfast—'Hey, waitress, gimme a cuppa Morning Roast, medium rare.'"

Both Phil and Roberts chuckled appreciatively.

"What about *my* name?" said Phil.

"Java? I *personally* liked it a lot," said Roberts. "It has a good old-fashioned macho image, but I think they're looking at demographics a little more upscale. I think they're leaning toward Morning Roast right now."

"Hey, what the hell," said Tony. "They want to call it Axle Grease, *I* give a good crap? It's only advertising, right?"

Phil sensed Tony's attitude would either greatly impede his advancement in advertising or else carry him straight to the top.

"Do you happen to know what they decaffeinate the coffee with, Ralph?" said Phil.

"I don't know," said Roberts. "I guess they use whatever is most commonly used in the industry. Why do you ask?"

"Well, we have a new baby," said Phil. "And while my wife was pregnant we were very careful not to let her drink anything that could've caused birth defects, like caffeine. But then I learned there are several processes of decaffeination, and not all of them are safe."

"Yeah," said Roberts.

"The best one is the Swiss water process," said Phil, "which was developed by Nestlé. It doesn't add any chemicals to the beans, but it's very expensive, so not many companies use it. A cheaper method, also safe, uses ethyl acetate. The worst one uses methylene chloride, which is an animal carcinogen."

"No shit?" said Tony. "You could get cancer from decaffeinated coffee?"

"Only if you're a laboratory mouse," said Roberts.

"I'd just like to know what process of decaffeination our client uses," said Phil.

"I'll check into it," said Roberts, "but I'm sure Consolidated Foods uses something safe."

"Why would you be sure of *that?*" said Phil.

Roberts and Tony laughed, but Phil hadn't been joking.

"Just out of curiosity," said Phil, "did you submit Java to the client?"

"Not really," said Roberts. "They'd never buy it."

"If you like the name," said Phil, "I'd really appreciate your submitting it to them, even if you don't think they'd buy it."

"O.K., Pressman," said Roberts, "I'll submit it. What the hell."

The next day Roberts stopped by Phil's office.

"Well, I submitted Java to the ad manager of Consolidated Foods," he said.

"Did he like it?" said Phil.

"No," said Roberts.

"No?"

"No," said Roberts, "he fucking *loved* it!"

"Really? He *loved* it?" said Phil, breaking into surprised laughter.

"Fucking *loved* it," Roberts repeated, slapping Phil on the back. "If they go ahead with it, which I think they will, there might be a bonus in it for you."

"No kidding?" said Phil. "That's terrific!"

"To be honest with you, I never thought they'd go for it."

"Boy, that's really great," said Phil. "Hey, did you find out what they use to decaffeinate the coffee?"

Roberts shook his head.

"What's the matter, Pressman," he said, "can't you just accept good news?"

CHAPTER 15

AT NANNY'S SUGGESTION Julie had spent a frustrating day with an obscene-looking breast pump, trying to express enough milk out of her breasts into a bottle so that Phil could give Harry his late-night feeding and allow Julie to get enough sleep to produce more milk.

Phil didn't mind giving Harry his late bottle. In short order he'd gotten the process down to a routine so slick he could do it without fully waking up. And Harry was so sleepy at that hour Phil could cuddle him and ponder the notion that he held in his arms a person who would one day borrow money from him and lust after women.

Julie's milk was still not flowing freely. Between Harry's voracious nursing and the forced suction of the breast pump to fill the relief bottle, her nipples were sore and beginning to crack. It was a nice change for her today to be able to talk to Phil about his success in naming the new coffee and to be able to focus on something other than milk.

Phil poured them a couple of glasses of wine to celebrate, but Julie was reluctant to drink while she was breast-feeding, and so he drank alone.

33

The wine made Phil a little light-headed, and he bent down to kiss her. Julie started to respond, but when he slipped his tongue between her lips she withdrew.

"What's the matter?" he whispered.

"Nothing."

"No, tell me," he said. "How come you pulled away?"

She sighed.

"Oh, you know. If I get too turned on then I'm going to want to make love, and . . ."

"And . . . ?"

"And it's too *soon*, Phil. I don't think my episiotomy is healed yet."

"Let's find out," said Phil, gently pushing her down on the bed.

"Phil, come on, that isn't fair."

"Fair? What's fair? We haven't made love in over eight weeks. I *want* you, Julie."

"I want you too, Phil, but it's just too soon."

"O.K.," he said, releasing her.

CHAPTER 16

ON ONE OF NANNY'S DAYS OFF they took Harry to a diner for dinner. Harry was still dining only on what he could extract from his mom's breasts, but Phil and Julie were anxious to get out of the house. The prospect of taking Harry to a good restaurant where the management might not be so tolerant of his prolonged crying was less than appealing, so a diner was a good compromise.

They arrived at the diner with all their gear—stroller, diaper bag, toys and so on, and Phil recalled how, before their baby's birth, he used to pity parents who traveled like this.

Shortly after they were seated in their booth, Harry decided he was hungry and began wailing to be fed. Without taking any care to keep herself covered, Julie whipped out her breast and stuffed it into Harry's mouth.

Phil had seen women nurse babies in public before and, try as he might, he'd never been able to glimpse any flesh. If anyone had been looking in Julie's direction tonight, they would have seen a lot. Julie hadn't yet gotten the hang of public nursing.

While Harry was attempting to extract sustenance from Julie's sluggishly flowing breasts, a young couple sat down in the adjoining booth and lit up cigarettes. Phil, who detested asking strangers in public places to do things, detested even more the idea of exposing his brand-new son's brand-new lungs to smoke. After a brief internal battle Phil stood up and walked over to the smoking couple.

"Forgive me," said Phil, "but we have a newborn baby in the next booth there, and I'm really worried about exposing him to smoke. Would you mind very much if I asked you to put out your cigarettes?"

The man and woman looked at Phil and, without a word, guiltily extinguished their smokes. Phil thanked them and went back to his own booth. Well, he thought, that was easy enough, but what would I have done if it hadn't been a polite young couple but two tough truckers?

When Harry was finished nursing, he stopped sucking on Julie's nipple and began to play with it.

"I don't think you're supposed to let him *play* with it," Phil whispered, looking nervously around to see if anyone was getting free peeks at his wife's breast.

"Hey, Harry, this isn't a toy here," said Julie, but Harry was clearly more interested in playing than nursing.

Julie put her breast away and Harry resumed crying, but when Julie pulled it back out he still wanted only to play with it. Phil wanted to play with it, too, and recalled a time when he hadn't considered his wife's breasts to be his son's territory.

When Harry's crying became oppressive, Phil picked him up and began to pace around the diner. Two teenaged girls in a booth at the end of the diner asked to hold him. Fearful of exposing him to irresponsible teenaged germs but not wishing to seem a bad sport, Phil compromised by holding the baby out for them to examine. Although Harry continued to whimper, the girls fussed over him and confessed how much they craved babies of their own.

"Babies are cute, but they're really a lot of work," said Phil, "believe me."

The girls said they didn't mind the work. Phil tried to envision the teenaged girls as harried moms who averaged three hours of sleep per night, bouncing colicky babies who wouldn't stop screaming.

"I really think you ought to wait awhile," said Phil.

"How long?" said the prettier of the two.

"Twenty or twenty-five years," said Phil seriously.

CHAPTER 17

THE PSYCHIATRIC RESIDENT walked into the room and saw that the man in the bed was sitting up and looking out the window. Since the man in the bed had previously shown little interest in doing anything but lying on his back and staring at the ceiling, the resident felt this to be an encouraging sign.

"Well well," said the resident, "and how are we today, Mr. Parsons?"

The man turned and looked at the resident with great interest.

"I can, of course, only speak for myself," said the man, "but I am smashing, absolutely smashing."

"Excellent," said the resident, consulting his metal clipboard and making the quick notation "smshng."

"Only one thing bothers me," said the man. "Well, two, actually."

"And what would those be?" said the resident, scribbling "2 thngs. bthr. hm." on his metal clipboard.

"Your stethoscope, for one," said the man.

"My stethoscope bothers you?" said the resident, scribbling "stethscp."

"Yes," said the man.

"What bothers you about my stethoscope?" said the resident.

"It bothers me that you drape it casually over the back of your neck and that it could slide off at any moment and fall to the floor and break, whereas if you merely suspended it from your neck by the earpieces, which is a much much logical way to transport it, it would always be safe and in place and ready for use."

"I see," said the resident. "And, uh, what is the second thing which bothers you?"

"Psychiatric residents who come in and ask me how 'we' are and who try to act casual and chatty while furtively scribbling notes on their clipboards," said the man.

CHAPTER 18

PHIL AND JULIE, who'd been raised to treat everybody as equals, were embarrassed at the idea of giving people orders, so they weren't definite enough when telling Nanny what to do. Consequently, Nanny felt free to do what she saw fit.

Although Julie was willing to submit to demand-feeding—nursing the baby whenever he was hungry—Nanny instituted a strict schedule of feedings four hours apart. Julie agreed to follow the schedule because Nanny seemed to know what was best for Harry.

Phil and Julie were inclined to pick the baby up every time he cried, but Nanny forbade it. When they forgot and did it anyway, she clucked her tongue. When they played with him, she hovered disapprovingly, which took a good deal of the spontaneity out of the activity.

Nanny's standards for cleanliness in the house were higher even than their own. She spent every moment she wasn't taking care of Harry vacuuming couches and carpeting, plumping up pillows, Windexing and Soft-Scrubbing windows, mirrors, coffee tables, sinks, tubs, toilets and chrome faucets to streak-free shines, often shooing Phil and Julie out of their chairs or off the couch to do it.

Nanny was shocked at what Phil and Julie ate and shamed them into a high-protein diet that included chicken, fish and shellfish, raw fruits and vegetables, and excluded steaks, roast beef, hamburgers, hot dogs, chili, tacos, pizza, ice cream, brownies and most of their favorite foods. They groused about the restrictions, but they admired the results.

"I hate to admit it," said Phil, "but I've been feeling pretty damned healthy of late."

"Yeah," said Julie, "me too."

"I guess she must really know something about nutrition after all," said Phil.

"And housecleaning," said Julie. "As much as I hate her anal compulsiveness about dirt and disorder, I have to admit she's a dynamite housekeeper."

Phil nodded.

"And," he said, "you have to admit she's great with Harry. She always seems to know just what he wants, and when she holds him he never cries."

"She *is* great with Harry," said Julie, and after a moment her face grew sad. "Maybe even a little *too* great."

"What do you mean?" said Phil.

She sighed and shook her head.

"Tell me," said Phil.

"Well," said Julie, "I don't like it that my son doesn't stop crying when I pick him up, that he only stops when *Nanny* picks him up, you know?"

"Mmmm."

"I mean," she said, "I sometimes feel as though he likes her better than he does me."

"That's foolish," said Phil.

"Why is it foolish?"

"Harry is *your* son, not Nanny's," he said. "Don't you think he knows that?"

Julie shook her head.

"No, Phil, I don't. I'm really beginning to feel he thinks *Nanny* is his mother."

"Well then," said Phil, "you simply haven't been reading the literature."

"What literature?"

"The books I bought you—*The First Twelve Months of Life* and all the others. They say the baby knows his mother from birth by her smell. I assure you Harry knows you're his mother—by your smell, if nothing else."

"Well, *that's* certainly reassuring," she said sarcastically.

"My God, Julie," he said, "you nurse him every four *hours*— how can he forget you?"

"I don't know," she said. "I'm not even nursing him well. Maybe if I had more milk I'd feel I was a better mother and worthier of his love."

Phil got up and went over to her and put his arms around her.

"Honey, please don't start again about the milk. The volume of milk you produce is not the measure of your worth as a mother. You're not supposed to be a goddam cow."

"I know that, but . . ."

"But nothing. *You* are the kid's mother, not Nanny—he knows that as well as I do. You're the only one who may be in doubt."

"I don't know," she said. "I hope you're right."

CHAPTER 19

DESPITE THEIR MISGIVINGS the quality of their lives since Nanny's arrival had definitely improved. Harry was crying less. They were getting valuable time away from him. They were getting time to sleep. Not enough, perhaps, but more than before.

They were still not making love. There was a good deal of guilt and apprehension associated with their lack of lovemaking. They had tried to do it twice. Both times Julie had to make Phil stop because it was too painful. Nothing that either of them had read in the guidebooks or heard from doctors or from friends who had babies themselves had prepared them for this.

They felt there was something wrong with them, yet it was clear that Julie's vagina was much tighter now than it had been before the episiotomy. It was as if she were a virgin again, only more so. When friends winked and asked if their sex life had returned to normal, they were reluctant to do anything but wink back and say yes, thereby perpetuating the myth.

One evening before dinner Phil and Julie were playing with Harry on the living room couch. Julie was trying to get him to smile by coaxing him and touching his chin. Phil was holding up a toy bunny he'd bought, whisking it out of sight, then returning it to Harry's field of vision. Harry seemed to find this activity amusing.

Nanny stood a few paces off, observing.

"At this age," said Nanny, "if you return an object to his field of vision within two and a half seconds, he'll remember it."

"Two and a half *seconds?*" said Julie.

"That's how long his memory is now," said Nanny.

Julie turned to Phil.

"That's just three seconds less than *yours*, honey," she said.

Phil was changing Harry's diapers. He noticed that Harry's penis was standing erect. Without warning, a stream of urine arced out of Harry's penis and directly into Harry's open mouth. The amazed baby burst into tears. Phil laughed and tried to soothe Harry as he dried him off.

Phil had developed several copy lines for the On A Clear Day print ads, but so far Ralph Roberts hadn't responded to any of them. He fiddled with the idea of a window so clean it was "pane-less," with the line "No pane, no gain," which made no sense at all; with the line "Through a glass darkly," which went nowhere; with the line "On a clear day you can see forever," which spelled out the title of the theme song the sponsor had paid big bucks to use in TV commercials, but this was a print ad. He came up with a promotion based on cleaning eyeglasses, and the line "No more specks on your specs," but he realized he was getting desperate.

He worked at the desk in the living-dining room while Harry slept, and worried that he would not be able to come up with a copy line that Ralph Roberts liked, worried that he would be fired and not be able to pay their rent or Nanny's salary, worried that Harry would suffocate in his sleep. Several times a night Phil leaned over Harry's cradle to listen for his tiny breathing.

CHAPTER 20

EARLY ONE EVENING Phil was standing in the kitchen, fixing himself a vodka tonic. From the baby's bathroom he heard the joyous, splashy sounds of Nanny giving Harry his evening bath. Phil yearned to be part of warm domestic scenes like this, and so, without knocking, he opened the bathroom door and stepped inside.

He should have knocked. Directly ahead of him were Harry and Nanny. The splashing had stopped. Both Harry and Nanny were in the tub. Both Harry and Nanny were naked. Both Harry and Nanny had turned to stare at him. Nanny met his gaze coolly, making no move to cover herself.

Phil stared open-mouthed at Nanny's unexpectedly voluptuous body. Images of her smooth, bath-moist, private flesh burned themselves forever into his retinas—her surprisingly full and beautifully shaped breasts, her surprisingly firm pink nipples, her surprisingly flat stomach, the thick black muff of her pubic hair lurking below the water line like a giant sea urchin.

Stammering apologies, Phil backed awkwardly out of the room and pulled the door shut behind him. He stood outside the bathroom door, trying to catch his breath, for suddenly he was finding it difficult to breathe. Coming upon the strange woman's nakedness so suddenly had produced in him a jarring and dizzying reaction.

He had unwittingly committed a severe invasion of her privacy. But what was she doing naked in the tub with his son in the first place? He wondered whether there was something going on that shouldn't be, something unclean, something kinky, something perverted, like the sick people who sexually abuse children in daycare centers.

No. He knew Nanny's credentials. He'd seen her letters of recommendation. He'd observed her in action—not for long, it

42

was true, but long enough to know she wasn't a child molester! Besides, if she had been doing anything of which she was ashamed, she'd surely have locked the bathroom door, wouldn't she? And when he walked in on her, she would have acted upset instead of the way she had, which was totally open and innocent and as if *he* were the intruder, which, in fact, he had been.

And yet. And yet, taking a bath with a baby *was* a bit on the peculiar side. Well, maybe it wasn't. Julie had taken the baby into the tub in their own bathroom to cuddle and play only the other day. But Julie was his mother, and Nanny was his nanny. Any way you looked at it, the entire business was very strange.

He wondered why Nanny had left the door unlocked. He wondered why she hadn't made any move to at least cover her nakedness when Phil walked in on her. He wondered at the look she'd given him that he'd backed away from, stammering apologies as he fled. He had seen in her manner something that had unnerved him. Perhaps it was a deliberate invitation. Perhaps she had set the whole thing up to be provocative.

No, it couldn't be. It was too preposterous. Until this moment Nanny was one of the least sexual women he had ever met. Indeed, everything about her discouraged rather than invited familiarity. Why, she'd even snubbed poor Julie's innocent invitation to eat breakfast with them, explaining that servants never ate with their employers. Well, servants who didn't *eat* with their employers certainly didn't *sleep* with them!

No, whatever the explanation for Nanny's appearance in the tub with Harry, it surely wasn't sexual. The problem was, Phil would no longer be able to look at Nanny clothed and not remember what she looked like naked.

He wondered what he could tell Julie about the incident, how much of it could be revealed to her without having her guess how aroused it had made him. He knew how unreasonably jealous she could become in the best of times, and these were surely not the best of times.

He vowed to tell Nanny there would be no more naked baths

with Harry and let the matter drop till the following morning, hoping it would cool enough in his brain to make it possible for him to mention it casually to both women.

But by the following morning he realized that waiting even overnight to discuss it with Julie could be suspicious. She'd want to know why he hadn't told her immediately, would guess why he hadn't, and her old jealousies, the jealousies which almost wrecked their relationship in college, would return again. He decided not to mention the incident to Julie at all. He would figure out a way to mention it to Nanny.

CHAPTER 21

PHIL had been trying to think of a tactful way to tell Nanny not to bathe with Harry, but he couldn't seem to get the wording right. Maybe it was because he was still feeling guilty at bursting in on her as he had.

He encountered her in the kitchen the following morning when she returned from her grocery-shopping expedition with the baby. He was uncomfortable and averted his eyes.

Maybe if he dealt with the invasion of privacy issue first—he ought to say something to her about that, but he didn't know what. That he was sorry he'd walked in on her—but he wasn't. That he'd seen more of her body than he ever expected to—but it hadn't been enough.

He'd already apologized, probably more than he should have. Maybe the best thing to do was just try to forget about it.

But forgetting about it wasn't easy. He tried to catch glimpses of her when she wasn't looking. He gazed at her severely starched white uniform and tried to envision the softness that lay just beneath it, tried to envision first the thin slippery layers of underclothes, then the soft secret flesh with which he had become accidentally, fleetingly acquainted.

It was absurd for him to feel he now had some intimate tie, however tenuous, to this woman who appeared to repel all intimacy, yet that was what he felt. She did not appear to be the type of person who willingly permitted anyone but physicians—or babies—to see her unclothed. He doubted whether half a dozen men had ever seen as much of her as he had. He could not help feeling attached to her for that.

It was extremely unlikely that any grown woman these days was sexually inexperienced, yet Phil could not imagine this one with a lover. There seemed to be no warmth about her, no sensuality. If that were so, then why had he become so fixated upon her body?

The opacity of the starched cotton of her uniform made it difficult for Phil to make out the indentations which normally frame female undergarments. As Nanny bent over the baby's bassinet he hazarded a swift search for visible panty lines. He had just about located the legbands when he realized that Nanny had asked him a question and that it hadn't registered.

He lifted his gaze to meet hers and reddened, caught like a schoolboy.

"I'm sorry," he said.

She looked at him with interest.

"*Are* you?" she said.

It was not a conventional reply. It was not a correct response to his implied request to repeat the question.

"Uh, I meant that I hadn't heard what you asked me," he said.

A pause.

"Hadn't you?" she said.

"No," he said, "I hadn't."

"I shouldn't wonder," she said.

45

It was not warm in the room, but perspiration prickled his temples. He decided to begin again.

"You asked me a question, didn't you?" he said.

"I did indeed."

"And I didn't hear you," said Phil.

"No, you didn't."

Nothing else appeared to be forthcoming.

"Would you mind repeating what you asked me?" he said, perspiration trickling into his eyes.

Her gaze never wavered. He could not imagine what she was thinking. There was more electricity in the air than in the baseboard outlet.

"I *would* mind, actually," she said, and turned back to the bassinet.

Phil stood there stupidly for a moment, then walked lamely out of the room.

CHAPTER 22

PHIL went to the desk and took out Nanny's letters of recommendation and reread them. The first one was from the dermatologist in Palm Beach, Florida:

To Whom It May Concern:

Miss Luci Redman has been in my employ for a period of three years. During that time she was responsible for the care of our infant and for the running of the household in general. Her duties included shopping for food and preparing the meals and cleaning the house.

We have found Miss Redman to be without peer in all of her duties, and were extremely sorry to see her go.

Sincerely,
Harold A. Millman, M.D.

The second was from the investment banker in Detroit, Michigan:

Dear Sir or Madam:

This is to verify that Miss Luci Redman was employed to run our household and be a nanny to our infant son for a period of two and one half years.

During such time she was a tireless worker, an exceptional house-cleaner and caretaker for our child, and she treated the baby as if he were her own.

I do not know what we would have done without Luci Redman. We were extremely sorry to see her leave, and envy her next employers.

Yours very truly,
William R. Parsons

Treated the baby as if he were her own, did she? Phil chuckled grimly. I'll *bet* she did, he thought.

The third letter was from the president of the oil company in Houston, Texas:

To Whom It May Concern:

I have the very great pleasure to recommend Miss Luci Redman for whichever job she chooses to accept in the fields of housekeeping and infant care.

Miss Redman has proven to be a most valuable employee and we were privileged to have had her for a nanny and a housekeeper. Should you desire further information about Miss Redman, please do not hesitate to call.

Sincerely yours,
Robert T. Conroy

O.K., Conroy, thought Phil, since you've volunteered. He reached for the phone and placed a person-to-person call to Conroy in Houston.

The operator unthinkingly announced the call as collect, and Phil, embarrassed and irritated, hastened to correct her. The operator was embarrassed to be wrong and irritated to be corrected and said something snotty to Phil. The oilman's secretary said that Mr. Conroy wasn't in, and Phil had to content himself with leaving his name and number, which the angry operator almost didn't allow him to do.

Phil called the dermatologist in Florida and then the investment banker in Detroit. and didn't reach them either.

That night he got home numbers for all three from Long Distance Information. There was no answer at the oilman's house in Houston or at the dermatologist's in Palm Beach, which was strange because they both had babies, and the investment banker's number in Detroit produced a recording which said that the number had been disconnected at the customer's request, whatever that meant.

The next day Phil called the oilman station-to-station and asked the secretary to be put through to Mr. Conroy.

"What is this in reference to?" said the secretary.

"Well," said Phil, "Mr. Conroy gave his name as reference for a nanny he once employed, and I just wanted to verify his praise of her in the letter I read."

There was a longish pause on the other end.

"I am sure," said the secretary, "that Mr. Conroy stands behind whatever he wrote, sir."

"Yes," said Phil, "but there were just a few things that I wanted to clarify about her that weren't in the letter."

"How soon were you planning on hiring this nanny?" said the secretary.

"Well, uh, I already hired her," said Phil, aware how asinine this must make him sound, "but—"

"If you've already hired her, then why do you need to find out anything from Mr. Conroy?" said the secretary reasonably.

"It's too . . . complicated to explain," said Phil. "I wonder if I might speak to Mr. Conroy personally."

"Mr. Conroy is in conference," said the secretary. "If you'd like to leave your name and number, I'll see that he gets back to you."

Phil gave his name and number again, knowing there wasn't the remotest chance that Conroy would get back to him. He was stupid to say he'd already hired her. Why did he have to say that?

He called Parsons, the investment banker, station-to-station and asked to speak to him.

"Can you tell me what this is in reference to?" said the banker's secretary.

"Someone I'm thinking of hiring has given Mr. Parsons as a reference," said Phil. "I just wanted to check her out."

"If you give me your name and number, I'll be glad to give Mr. Parsons the message," she said.

Phil gave his name and number a second time and knew he wouldn't hear from the investment banker either. He dialed the dermatologist and asked to speak to him.

"May I know what this is in reference to?" said the receptionist.

"No," said Phil.

"Excuse me?"

"What I mean to say," said Phil, "is that I have a severe skin eruption in a rather embarrassing place and I'd prefer to speak to the doctor directly about it."

"Would you like an appointment?" said the receptionist.

"Well, yes," said Phil, "but I really do need to talk to the doctor beforehand."

Phil allowed the receptionist to make an appointment for him for three weeks from Thursday, and then she put him through to Dr. Millman.

"This is Dr. Millman," said a grave voice.

"Dr. Millman, my name is Phil Pressman . . ."

"Yes . . ."

"I need to talk to you about Luci Redman."

Total silence greeted this announcement.

"Dr. Millman?"

"My receptionist said that you had a question about a skin eruption," said Dr. Millman evenly.

"I know," said Phil. "But I also need to talk to you about Luci Redman. You did write her a letter of recommendation, did you not? I mean, you are *that* Dr. Millman, aren't you?"

Another silence.

"I'm sorry, Mr., uh . . . ?"

"Pressman, Phil Pressman . . ."

"Mr. Pressman, we are very busy here," said Dr. Millman. "My practice is such that it is all I can do to see the patients who need my medical help. If you are having a genuine dermatological problem, I shall be glad to treat you at the time the receptionist has given you, but that is all I can—"

"Dr. Millman, couldn't you just answer a few questions about Luci Redman?" said Phil. "Just a few? It would mean a great deal to me."

Yet another silence.

"Dr. Millman?"

"Mr. Pressman," said Dr. Millman, "the individual you have mentioned to me is not someone whom I can recommend. And now I really must get back to my medical practice."

Click.

Phil stood stupidly looking at the disconnected phone in his hand.

CHAPTER 23

JULIE was trying to nurse Harry and he wasn't having any of it. She kept trying to stuff her breast into Harry's mouth and Harry kept spitting it out.

"Harry, do you know how many men have *fought* to suck on what you're spitting out?" said Julie. "I mean literally *fought?*"

Harry began to cry.

"He isn't taking my breast anymore," said Julie.

"I thought he *was*," said Phil. "I thought your flow was getting better and he was really starting to nurse well."

"It was getting better for a while," she said, "but then he stopped taking my breast and now the flow is beginning to dry up. That's what happens if the baby isn't sucking enough—it dries up. And then there isn't any milk left and you have to stop nursing."

She joined Harry in tears.

"I'm sorry I'm crying again, Phil," she said, trying to stop and not succeeding. "I wanted to nurse him for at least three months. At least long enough for him to get the nutrients and the immunities that you get from breast milk. But now I'm not going to be able to. Now I'm going to have to put him on the bottle."

Phil tried to comfort both his wife and his son.

"You can still try to get him to nurse," he said.

Julie shook her head.

"I *have* tried," she said. "He won't take it anymore. Why *should* he—the nipples on the relief bottles you give him at night flow so much easier. Why should he struggle with *my* nipples when he can get it so much easier from the other ones?"

"Well, let's say we have to convert him to the bottle," said Phil. "That would certainly make your life easier, wouldn't it? If you didn't have to be on call for breast-feeding every four hours you could sleep more at night and go out more during the day. You know, I don't think putting him on the bottle would be the worst thing in the world for you."

"Yes it would," she said.

"Why?"

"Because my breast-feeding is the last link I have to him, Phil," she said quietly and began crying again.

"Why do you say that?" he said, trying to console her.

"Don't you see how he acts with me? With us? Look at him. He barely tolerates me, Phil. He thinks *Nanny* is his mother, not me."

"Come on, Julie, don't be ridiculous. I've told you many times, the baby clearly knows who his mother is. The baby—"

"The *baby*," she said, interrupting, her voice edging into hysteria, "cries when you or I pick him *up*. The baby *stops* crying when *Nanny* picks him up. The baby and everybody else in this house is totally under that woman's control!"

"Then we have to have this out with her."

"What do you mean?"

"We have to have a meeting," said Phil. "We have to tell her who's the boss in this house."

"She already *knows* who the boss is," said Julie. "That's the trouble."

"Well then, we'll just have to change the ground rules, that's all."

Harry's crying was edging into hysteria.

"It's too late," said Julie defeatedly.

"It's not too late," said Phil decisively. "O.K., we made a few mistakes with her starting off, I admit that. We got off on the wrong foot with her, was the problem. We weren't used to servants and we were a little shy about asking her to do what we wanted, and so she took advantage of the situation. But if we have a conference and spell out new guidelines, she's going to toe the mark, you'd better believe it. She's either going to shape up or ship out."

"You really think we can change her?"

"I do. Nanny is a tyrant, Julie. Tyrants are like little kids throwing a tantrum. A little kid throwing a tantrum just wants to be stopped. If we stop Nanny she'll be grateful to us."

Julie looked at him dubiously.

"You really believe this?"

"Absolutely," said Phil. "Nanny is our *employee*, Julie. We are her *employers*. She is our *servant*. I know we don't feel comfortable with that word in this country, but *she* does. She understands that word very well. She'll either do as we say or we'll get rid of her."

Julie mopped her eyes.

"I just figured out what the problem really is," she said.

"What?"

"I just now figured it out," she said. "Nanny dominates us because she senses it fulfills a deep longing in us."

"You're insane," said Phil.

"No I'm not," said Julie. "You love strong maternal figures like Nanny because your mother was very strong—Nanny reminds you of her. And *I* probably love them because my mother was so weak—Nanny is the strong mommy I never had."

Phil closed his eyes and massaged his temples with the tips of his fingers.

"Julie, when are you going to wake up and discover you're an interior decorator and not a shrink?" said Phil, but he suspected she was on to something.

CHAPTER 24

THE MEETING took place in the living-dining room after Harry finally fell asleep. Phil and Julie sat on the couch facing Nanny. Everybody had very serious looks on their faces.

"We have called this meeting, Nanny," said Phil, "because Mrs. Pressman and I find that there are a number of things about our situation here which displease us."

"I see," said Nanny.

"Things which displease us and which we need to have changed," said Phil.

"I see," said Nanny.

It's going to work, thought Phil in surprise, it's really going to work—she is actually taking this seriously.

"First of all," said Phil, "Mrs. Pressman and I feel that you do not behave toward us in an appropriate manner. We are your employers, and you are our employee, and we would like to see that reflected in your behavior.

"Second," said Phil, "in the future we would like you to buy and cook for us food that *we* choose and not food that *you* select for us."

He looked to see whether Nanny was having the furious reaction he'd feared she might and was vastly relieved to see she had no reaction at all.

"Finally," said Phil, "there is Harry. We require that he be fed and bathed and attended to in the manner that *we* and not you deem best for him—regardless of your own, I'm sure, quite educated views on baby care."

Phil turned to Julie.

"Do you have anything to add, Julie?" he said.

"No," she said.

Phil turned back to Nanny.

"Do you have anything you'd like to say?" he said.

Nanny looked blankly at Phil. Jesus, he thought, I've knocked the stuffing out of her—she's absolutely speechless.

"Nanny," Phil repeated slowly, "do you have anything you'd like to say?"

"Yes," she said in a flat voice, "I do. You say you wish your child to be fed and bathed and attended to in the manner that you deem best for him, Mr. Pressman."

"Yes."

"What manner would that be, exactly?"

"Excuse me?" said Phil.

"What manner do you deem best for him?" said Nanny. "I'm anxious to know that."

"Ah," said Phil, temporarily thrown by the question and, as he learned to do in college, stalling for time by rephrasing the question. "Well, the manner in which we deem best for him to be fed and bathed and attended to is the manner in which we, uh, were taught by the various instructors in our Lamaze classes and, uh, in our breast-feeding classes, and in our classes in the hospital on baby care."

Nanny stared straight ahead for a moment, and then continued in the same flat voice.

"And that is as specific as you can be?" she said.

"For now," said Phil.

"I see," she said. "Well then, you have told me of your dissatisfactions. Now I should like to tell you some of mine."

Phil looked at Julie.

"All right," he said, "I suppose that's fair."

"Good," said Nanny. "First, your knowledge of babies and their proper care is so meager it is astonishing the child was still alive when I arrived. It is, in fact, only due to my arrival that the child survives to this day. I can promise you that any attempt to institute your own procedures in lieu of mine will have disastrous consequences on the child's health.

"Second," said Nanny, "the room in which I am currently sleeping is so woefully insufficient in size as to be claustrophobic. I do not know how you can in good conscience expect anyone to live there. It is only out of deference to the child that I remain here at all.

"Third, I am doing a more than competent job taking care of your child and keeping your house, under conditions which would send any other self-respecting British nanny screaming into the night. I resent being reprimanded, and I trust it shall never happen again."

Nanny stood up, nodded pleasantly in their direction and turned toward her room.

"And now, if you will excuse me," she said, "I believe I am off duty."

Nanny walked briskly out of the room.

CHAPTER 25

IT TOOK several seconds for Phil and Julie to come back to life.

"What in the name of Christ was *that?*" said Phil. "I mean, can you tell me what that was?"

Julie looked as if she were trying to decide whether to laugh or cry. She started to speak, not knowing quite what she was going to say.

"I think . . . that our nanny has . . . a few reservations about the job," was what she finally said, and began laughing so violently that Phil had to pound her on the back, and then he was laughing as well, and it was the perfect release of all the tension that had been building up for the past few weeks.

The laughter died out, and then it began again, more forcefully than before, and then that, too, was spent and they grew silent.

"Well," said Phil, "I guess our initial doubts about the woman have proven accurate."

Phil was just about to tell Julie about the call to Dr. Millman and how Millman had said he couldn't recommend Nanny, but then he realized he'd have to explain why he'd placed the call in the first place, and that would necessitate telling her about coming upon Nanny and Harry in the bath and why he hadn't told her about it until now, and he decided it wasn't worth it.

"Do you want to fire her or should I?" said Julie.

"I'll do it," said Phil.

"O.K.," said Julie. "I think you'd better do it now, though. She can wait till tomorrow to move out—assuming she's able to stand the claustrophobia of her tiny bedroom for one more night."

Phil chuckled and stood and started to go.

"Phil?" said Julie soberly, halting his forward momentum.

"Yeah, babe?"

A sigh.

"Are we going to be able to make it without her?"

CHAPTER 26

PHIL stood outside Nanny's bedroom door a moment, trying to put together the words with which to fire her. He'd never fired anyone before in his life, and although she richly deserved firing for the manner in which she'd spoken to them, he was still well aware of how good she had been with Harry.

Phil knocked on Nanny's door.

"Yes?" said Nanny's voice.

"It's Mr. Pressman," said Phil.

A pause.

"Yes, Mr. Pressman?"

"I'd like to speak with you a moment, if that's all right?"

Another pause.

"Come in, Mr. Pressman."

Phil turned the knob and entered the admittedly small bedroom. Nanny stood on the far side of the bed, facing the door.

"What is it you wish to discuss?" said Nanny.

"First of all," said Phil, "I think I ought to tell you that I recently called one of your references, Dr. Millman. He told me he couldn't give you a recommendation."

"I shouldn't wonder," she said.

"Excuse me?" said Phil.

"Dr. Millman suggested that I sleep with him," she said. "When

I refused, he became livid. I should be rather surprised if he had any desire to recommend me."

"Then why did he write you that letter of recommendation?" said Phil.

"He wrote it when I first gave notice," said Nanny. "Before he made his suggestion that we sleep together."

"I see," said Phil. "Well. In any case, the fact is, Nanny, that, although you've been quite good with the baby, we find that the way you have been with *us* makes it no longer possible to employ you."

Nanny looked at him thoughtfully a moment, then reached behind her and unzipped her uniform. Phil stared at her in disbelief.

"What are you doing?" he said.

In reply she slipped first one arm and then the other out of her uniform and pulled it over her head.

"We can talk about this tomorrow morning when it's more convenient," he said hastily, turning toward the door.

Nanny stepped swiftly to the door and shut it before he could step through it.

"It will never be any more convenient than it is right now," she said, smoothing the wrinkles of her white nylon slip down over her hips, blocking his exit.

This is not happening, Phil thought dizzily, I am hallucinating this.

"I think you'd better let me out of here," said Phil, again reaching for the door and again having his exit blocked. "And I think you'd better be gone tomorrow morning."

He saw for the first time an expression of uncertainty cross her face.

"Surely you're not serious," she said.

"Of course I'm serious," said Phil, absorbing the little composure she'd lost.

She looked at him a moment longer, then pushed her slip down over her hips and let it fall to the floor. There was an unobtrusive floral pattern on both her brassiere and her white nylon panties which the designer probably intended as a nod toward modesty, but since both garments were translucent Phil had no difficulty making out the darker shapes of her nipples and her pubic mound. He was light-headed and felt as though he were in a trance.

"Why are you doing this?" he said hoarsely.

"To change your decision."

"You're not changing it," he said. "You're reinforcing it."

With an oddly vulnerable smile on her face, Nanny stepped quite close to Phil. Her lips brushed his lips. He felt heat radiating from his cheeks and forehead and neck and he felt himself get hard.

He knew it was utter madness to stay in this room a moment longer, but the signals his brain was sending to his legs to walk weren't getting through. The channel was being blocked the way Lamaze breathing blocked messages of pain. It felt as if his body was being held in some sort of electromagnetic suspension.

Through a supreme effort of will he was finally able to lift one foot and move it closer to the door. And then the other. He was walking underwater with swim fins on his feet.

"I want this job, Mr. Pressman," she whispered. "I don't want to be fired."

Phil snorted.

"I'm serious," she said, caressing his face, pressing her warm lips against it. "I want to stay here. I may not have shown it, but I'm very fond of you. Of your family. I'll do anything to stay here. Anything at all."

"*Anything?*" he said.

"Anything," she said huskily.

"Even behave like a professional?" he said.

"If that's what it takes," she said, drawing back from him, cooling quickly from the rejection.

Amazingly, he thought he saw tears in her eyes.

He grasped the doorknob, tightened numb fingers around it, turned it clockwise and opened the door. He stepped unsteadily across the threshold, permitted himself one last look at the tall, voluptuous woman he was rejecting, then shakily pulled the doorknob shut behind him.

He was tremendously aroused. He had absolutely no idea what he was going to tell his wife.

CHAPTER 27

"So how did she take it?" said Julie, getting up from their bed in her pink flannel nightgown.

Phil walked unsteadily into their bathroom and began elaborately flossing his teeth.

"Not in the way you would have thought," said Phil, stalling for time.

"Really?" said Julie. "What happened?"

"Well, I don't think she took me seriously at first," said Phil, spitting into the sink. "Maybe she figured I was bluffing. Maybe she thought we couldn't do without her . . ."

"Yeah . . ." said Julie, coming into the bathroom.

"But then she finally realized I was serious," said Phil, squeezing a length of multi-hued Aqua-fresh toothpaste out onto his toothbrush.

"And what did she do then?" said Julie.

Phil was silent while he brushed his teeth for thirty seconds in the direction of growth, considering his story. Then he turned to face her.

"She broke down and wept," he said.

"You're *kidding* me!"

Phil shook his head.

"She broke down and wept like a baby," he said.

"I don't be-*lieve* it!" shrieked Julie delightedly, clapping her hands like a small child.

"At first," said Phil, emboldened by her reaction, "it was very satisfying, of course. Then it became sort of pathetic. She gave me this whole song-and-dance routine about how she wants this job, about how she doesn't want to be fired, about how she's really fond of us, how she'll do anything to stay, anything at all—that sort of thing. Anyway, the bottom line is she begged me for another chance."

"She *begged* you? Really?"

"Yep."

"And what did you tell her?" said Julie.

Phil filled the red plastic cup on the counter with water, took a swig, rinsed his teeth and spit into the sink.

"Julie, I am not totally without compassion. I am not a hard-hearted man. I told her she could have a second chance."

"You did?"

"She was so grateful she *kissed* me, Julie. The woman kissed me in gratitude!"

Julie shook her head in wonder.

"I don't believe it," she said. "I can't imagine Nanny kissing anybody."

"Well, she did kiss me," he said.

"God," she said. "That's amazing."

"I did make it very clear to her that if things didn't get *substantially* better in two weeks she'd have to leave," said Phil. "I hope that arrangement is O.K. with you, because if it isn't I'll go right back in there and tell her to get out *tonight*."

Julie shook her head.

"No no, that's fine," she said. "I'll just be very anxious to see how she behaves toward us now, that's all."

"So will I," said Phil. "Believe me, Julie, so will I."

CHAPTER 28

PHIL sat at his desk in his office at Sullivan, Stouffer, Cohn and McConnell, staring at the sheet of white paper in his typewriter and thinking.

If it had been difficult before for him to look at Nanny in her uniform without seeing her unclothed, it was now impossible. Images of Nanny nude and in various stages of undress inhabited his brain like bawdy lodgers.

His ambivalence about what had happened in Nanny's bedroom was monumental. He felt vaguely compromised by the experience, but congratulated himself for not succumbing to her advances.

If he gave in and had sex with her he knew exactly what would happen. The pleasure and excitement would be excruciating for about twenty minutes. Then he would swim in a thick soup of guilt for days until he could tolerate his own rottenness no longer.

To dissipate his guilt he would then begin to rationalize how Julie actually *deserved* being cheated on. He would dredge up old grievances, grievances from the early years of their relationship at the U. of I., grievances long since negotiated and deactivated, to prove his case. The more he could rationalize that she deserved being cheated on, the less worse he'd feel, until he had succeeded in whitewashing himself and tarring her beyond recognition.

This process he'd dubbed Retroactive Deserving, and the reason he knew so well how it worked was that he'd discovered himself using it back at the U. of I. when he'd been fooling around with other women and needed to stop hating himself for what he was doing.

He felt that the process of Retroactive Deserving, once begun, would be practically impossible to halt this time, until eventually his marriage was in tatters. Horny though he might be, he was not so horny that he was willing to jeopardize his relationship with Julie, whom he truly loved, for twenty minutes of ecstasy with his son's nanny.

He recalled Julie's theory that he was drawn to strong maternal women because they reminded him of his mother. He was loath to credit Julie's ubiquitous pop-psych theories, but he suspected she was right. Both Nanny and Mary Margaret Sullivan had a stronger than usual attraction for him.

His real mother had been not only strong and maternal, but unconsciously provocative as well. She had spent Phil's boyhood walking around their apartment in brassiere, panties, stockings and garters, leaving bedroom and bathroom doors ajar when she dressed, undressed, bathed or went to the toilet. She was too dangerous to be close to, and so Phil distanced himself from her as best he could, making fun of her to others at every opportunity to throw them off the track. No one would have guessed Phil's real feelings for her, with the possible exception of Julie. His adult obsession with Nanny mirrored the childhood one with his mom.

Because of his current obsession with Nanny, Phil seemed incapable of work, incapable of coming up with a single good idea for the On A Clear Day glass spray commercials. He was able to come up with plenty of bad ones: a pompous man in an office walking smack into a glass door that had just been sprayed with the client's product; Alice of *Alice in Wonderland* spraying a mirror, then walking through it; a woman spraying a window in winter and being able to see the scene outside in spring; an old man spraying a window and being able to see sepia images from his past; a little boy spraying a window and being able to see zappy images of the future; Clark Kent spraying and wiping his glasses, then suddenly able to see through a woman's clothing with X-ray vision; a woman executive spraying and wiping her glasses, putting them on, taking a look at her meek male secretary and exclaiming, "Why, Mr. Jeffries, you're . . . you're *beautiful.*"

Phil hated every idea he came up with. Worse yet, he felt unable to think of any others, even bad ones. The well seemed suddenly to have run dry. He was suffering from some fiendish sort of copywriter's block. He wondered whether it was a permanent condition. He wondered whether it would last long enough to get him fired.

CHAPTER 29

JULIE was amazed. Amazed, encouraged and even moved. The idea that Nanny actually wanted this job enough to beg for a second chance—actually broke down and *wept* in the process—was very encouraging.

It also said a lot to Julie about Nanny that she hadn't suspected, but should have, given her understanding of human behavior from when she'd studied it in college. It said a lot about Nanny's vulnerability. Julie knew several people who behaved in as superior and aggressive a fashion as Nanny—well, maybe not *quite* as superior and aggressive a fashion as Nanny—and most of them had revealed themselves at one time or another, however briefly, to be vulnerable and sensitive people who put on a tough exterior to avoid being hurt.

It was reassuring to know that even Nanny had feelings and needs and vulnerabilities and insecurities like everybody else. It was nice to know, in short, that Nanny was human.

CHAPTER 30

PHIL tried again to follow up on Nanny's references.

He called back Parsons, the investment banker, and asked to speak to him.

"Are you a client of Mr. Parsons, Mr. Pressman?" said the secretary.

"No, but I'd like to open an account."

"Who recommended you to Mr. Parsons?" said the secretary.

"Mr. . . . Johnson," said Phil, hoping Parsons had at least one client named Johnson.

"Mr. Emmet Johnson?"

"Yes, of course," said Phil. "But I really would like to speak to Mr. Parsons."

"If you like, I can open the account for you over the phone," said the secretary.

Phil took a deep breath.

"Listen, Miss," he said, "I have two hundred and fifty thousand dollars which I would like to invest. Mr. Johnson was quite enthusiastic in his recommendation of Mr. Parsons and I am willing to invest with him, and him alone. But if you are unable to put me through to him immediately I shall have to take my business to Shearson Lehman."

The secretary paused to consider this.

"Mr. Pressman, Mr. Parsons is temporarily on leave, but in his absence Mr. Thurston is handling his accounts. Mr. Thurston has just gotten off the phone and I can put you through to him right now."

"I don't *want* to be put through to Mr. Thurston," said Phil. "Mr. Johnson specifically recommended Mr. *Parsons*. When will Mr. Parsons return?"

"That's . . . difficult to say, sir," said the secretary. "He'll return as soon as he is able, I have no doubt. He hasn't felt too much like working since the tragedy, of course."

"The tragedy?"

"I'm afraid I have another call," said the secretary. "Would you like to speak with our Mr. Thurston?"

"Listen, I know this is a delicate time for Mr. Parsons," said Phil, "but I really must speak to him."

"I see," said the secretary.

"Do you have a number where he can be reached?" said Phil.

"I'm sorry, Mr. Pressman," said the secretary. "I have been specifically requested not to give out that information. Did you wish to speak to Mr. Thurston?"

"Look, I realize you have your orders, but it's really critical that I speak to Mr. Parsons," said Phil, realizing the futility of pursuing it any further. "Could you at least get a message to him for me? It's a personal message. It has nothing to do with my investments."

"I'll see what I can do, sir."

"Good," said Phil resignedly. "Tell Mr. Parsons that Mr. Pressman called. Tell him that I have employed Luci Redman based on reading his letter of recommendation, and that a situation has arisen in which I urgently need his advice. Will you tell him that?"

"Yes, sir."

"Did you get everything I told you, or do you want me to repeat it?"

An exasperated sigh.

"I got your message, Mr. Pressman."

"Thank you," said Phil.

CHAPTER 31

RALPH ROBERTS stopped by Pressman's office to see how he was
coming with the coffee and glass spray campaigns. Ralph liked the
young copywriter and wished the kid didn't have to put himself
through all the grief he obviously put himself through every time
he did a job.

"You got anything to show me yet?" said Ralph.

Pressman looked up and handed Ralph a sheaf of papers. Ralph
looked them over while Pressman waited nervously.

At the top of one page was the line: "At last, a decaf coffee with
all the perks left in." On another was a still shot from *Casablanca*
showing Bogart and Bergman looking into a full-length mirror.
With a magic marker Pressman had sketched a can of glass spray
into Bogart's hand, and a balloon above Bogart's head said "Here's
looking at *you*, kid."

"Now we're *getting* somewhere," said Ralph.

Pressman looked incredulous.

"You're serious?"

"Absolutely," said Ralph, "these are great."

"Thank God," said Pressman.

"You had doubts?"

"Yep," said Pressman, "you bet."

"I didn't," said Ralph.

"Thank you," said Pressman. "Tony's got some layouts on these he wants to show you."

"I'll stop by his office now."

"Good," said Pressman. "Listen, did you really find out anything about how they decaffeinate Java or not?"

Ralph shook his head. The kid had a wild hair about this decaf process that Ralph didn't understand.

"Don't *worry* about it," said Ralph. "I *told* you. It's all *right*."

"Then they don't use methylene chloride?" said Pressman.

"Has anybody ever told you you have an obsessive personality?" said Ralph.

"Actually, yes," said Pressman.

Ralph noticed a framed photo on Pressman's wall. Two women and a baby.

"That your wife and kid?" said Ralph.

"Yep."

"Very nice," said Ralph. "Who's the other gal?"

"The baby's nanny," said Pressman.

Ralph's eyes widened.

"Lucky baby," said Ralph.

"Yeah," said Pressman.

"Very strong face. Very good bones," said Ralph. "The body isn't a crying shame either."

"I hadn't noticed," said Pressman.

There was something a little too casual about Pressman's responses. Ralph wondered if Pressman was getting into the nanny's pants. Ralph continued to scrutinize the photo.

"I've often wondered," said Ralph carefully, "what it would be like to have a strange woman living under my roof, taking care of my kid. I mean I've often wondered how I'd handle it. You know what I mean?"

"No," said Pressman, "what do you mean?"

"I've often wondered if the temptation to sleep with her wouldn't become so overwhelming I just couldn't contain myself."

"I wouldn't know about that," said Pressman.

"Oh really?" said Ralph.

"No, I really wouldn't know about that."

Ralph smiled a sly smile.

"Come on, Phil," said Ralph. "Are you telling me you aren't even *tempted* to play hide-the-pepperoni with the gal in this picture?"

Pressman smiled at Ralph.

"Not even tempted," he said.

CHAPTER 32

PHIL was restless. He was vastly relieved that Roberts liked his ideas for the coffee and the glass spray ads, but it seemed to him that Roberts was being evasive about Java's decaffeination process. All he'd said both times Phil had asked him about it was that it was O.K. and not to worry about it. Phil *was* worried about it. He suspected that Consolidated Foods decaffeinated their coffee —*his* coffee, the coffee it was *his* responsibility to get people to buy and drink—with a chemical that caused cancer. He didn't see how he could be a party to that.

He wondered what would happen if he refused to work on the coffee account on moral grounds. He wondered if they'd simply take him off the account or if they'd fire him. He couldn't afford to be fired, especially now with the baby and all of their new expenses. But he also couldn't afford to participate in a campaign to convince people to drink something which might give them cancer.

He thought of going to Mary Margaret Sullivan with his dilemma. In the old days, he'd heard, when she started the agency, she'd had a very strong moral code. No cigarette or liquor accounts, no products that weren't the best in their respective fields. He knew she hadn't been able to hold the line on quality clients over the years as she'd hoped, he knew that some compromises had had to be made, but surely the notion of hawking a carcinogenic beverage had to be repugnant to her. Surely she had to sympathize with his feelings about that.

He stopped by the desk of Sullivan's secretary.

"When Ms. Sullivan is free I'd like to see her for a moment," said Phil.

"What is this in reference to?" said the secretary.

"I'd rather tell her myself," said Phil.

"No problem," said the secretary. "I should tell you, though, that she's very busy today, and tomorrow she's working at home, so if you *could* give me some idea of what it's about, it might help."

"O.K.," said Phil. "It's about cancer."

"Excuse me?" said the secretary.

"It's about a product I'm working on that I have reason to believe might be dangerous to the consumer's health."

"What product is that?" said the secretary.

"Java."

"Oh, I'm sure you needn't have any worries on *that* score," said the secretary.

"Well," said Phil with what he hoped was withering sarcasm, "I'm immensely relieved. I'm grateful for your reassurance."

"Don't mention it," said the secretary with a self-satisfied smile. "Will you still be wanting to see Ms. Sullivan?"

"Yes," said Phil.

"I'll see when the next available opening is," she said disappointedly.

CHAPTER 33

BEFORE he went down for his nap, Harry had been playing with his hair for security, pulling on it and crying at the pain.

Julie managed to loosen the tightly wound strands of hair from around the baby's fingers before inserting a pacifier into his mouth and putting him down on his stomach in the bassinet. Harry kept flailing around, throwing his head from side to side, smooshing his face into the mattress, dislodging the pacifier and then screaming because he'd lost it.

At length Nanny took over and got him settled down and to sleep, but the baby's crying had given Julie a throbbing headache. It felt as though the muscles in her upper back and neck had shrunk in the wash and were pulling her head down into her shoulders by degrees. It felt as though wet rawhide cords had been tied around her head and were drying in the sun's heat, tightening around her forehead and temples and crushing her skull.

Julie had taken two extra-strength Tylenols about three hours before, but the pain had hardly lessened at all, and now she wanted to take another dose. She wondered if it were safe. She wondered if it would somehow get into her milk and harm Harry.

Nanny was now in the kitchen, cooking. Nanny was a nurse. Nanny would tell her if it was all right to take more Tylenols.

"Nanny," said Julie, "I've got a really hideous headache. How often can I take extra-strength Tylenol?"

Nanny turned to look at her.

"Show me where it hurts," said Nanny.

Julie traced the pattern of pain around her head, down her neck, into her upper back.

"Come here," said Nanny.

Julie walked over to the sink where Nanny was peeling carrots. Nanny put her hands gently on both sides of Julie's head.

"Close your eyes," said Nanny.

Julie closed her eyes. Nanny began lightly massaging Julie's temples, then her forehead, then around her eyes.

"Turn around," said Nanny.

Julie turned around. Nanny continued her massaging, working her fingertips slowly down the back of Julie's neck, into the trapezius muscles between her neck and shoulders, and down around her shoulder blades.

"That hurts," said Julie.

"I shouldn't wonder," said Nanny. "You're tight as a drum."

The more Nanny massaged, the less it hurt, and Julie felt warmth begin to spread into the muscles that Nanny was manipulating. Slowly the muscles began to loosen up and the pain to subside.

"You're very good at that," said Julie gratefully.

"Thank you," said Nanny.

Julie was surprised and pleased that Nanny had said thank you. Julie wasn't certain she had heard Nanny accept many compliments before. In fact, Nanny had softened considerably since Phil had attempted to fire her. The change that had come over her was amazing. She must really have wanted this job a lot more than either of them had suspected.

"It's starting to feel better," said Julie. "I can't thank you enough."

"Would you like me to work some more on your back?" said Nanny.

"Well, sure," said Julie. "If it's not too much trouble, I mean."

"It's no trouble, dear," said Nanny. "And even if it were, I do work for you, don't I?"

"Yes," said Julie, "I suppose you do."

"Why don't you go and lie down on your bed," said Nanny, "and I'll really get to work on that back."

Julie went into her bedroom with Nanny following. Nanny helped Julie off with her sweater and blouse, then had her lie face down on the bed. She unhooked the back of Julie's nursing bra and began to manipulate the muscles of her back.

Julie had never felt anything like it before. True, she hadn't had many massages because of the expense—not more than three in her life, in fact—but she was certain that none of her masseuses had hands like Nanny's. Nanny's hands were the strongest and the gentlest hands that Julie had ever felt.

Nanny prodded and poked and pummeled and pulled and kneaded and stroked the flesh of Julie's upper and lower back until the warmth radiated upward and outward to all points of Julie's body and left it loose and relaxed and tingling. The headache had fled, chased by Nanny's magical fingertips, and in its place came a drowsy, dizzy feeling that was close to euphoria.

"Oh, Nanny." Julie sighed. "I've never had such a massage in my life. I feel wonderful."

"I'm glad, dear," said Nanny. "Would you like to sleep now?"

"Yes, Nanny, that would be wonderful."

Nanny covered Julie with a down comforter, patted her gently on the head, tiptoed out of the bedroom and closed the door behind her.

CHAPTER 34

AS THE TUB filled with water, Nanny gently undressed Harry and readied him for his bath. He was such a beautiful baby, and he so obviously loved his Nanny.

Nanny loved him too, had known she had a special rapport with him from the moment she'd first seen him on the day she interviewed for this job. He never cried when Nanny picked him up. Colic or no, Harry was not a difficult baby to care for. She lowered him into the warm water and began to soap his chubby little body, from his exquisitely intelligent face down to his delectable little penis.

The baby's mother was turning out to be quite a bit better than Nanny had thought she'd be. Mrs. Pressman was a beautiful woman with a good heart. All she really needed was a little mothering, a little loving. Well, mothering and loving just happened to be Nanny's specialties. Whatever Mrs. Pressman needed Nanny could supply—*would* supply—better than anyone on earth. Why, if Mrs. Pressman let her, she and Nanny would be thick as thieves in no time.

Mr. Pressman was the only imponderable. He seemed to vacillate between strength and passivity, between lust and prudery, between manhood and boyhood. She'd been surprised at his reaction to the flirtation in her bedroom. She suspected it had meant more to him than he let on. Mr. Pressman, too, needed love— just what kind she wasn't yet sure. Whatever kind he needed, though, she was certain she could supply it.

CHAPTER 35

TO PHIL'S AMAZEMENT, Nanny's behavior since his attempt to fire her had changed markedly. Her arrogance and rigidity had mellowed considerably. She still maintained a tight schedule in regard to baby care and housekeeping, but she was hardly domineering at all. At times she was almost deferential. Even more remarkably, something approaching warmth now flavored her communications to them.

Phil noticed that whenever his and Nanny's eyes met now, she smiled a sly, conspiratorial smile. She obviously realized he hadn't told Julie everything that had happened in her bedroom when he'd tried to fire her, and it was now a little secret that he and Nanny shared.

Phil found such secrets exciting. When he was going steady with Julie in college and seeing other girls on the sly, the sneaking around had been nearly as thrilling as the sex. For an honest man Phil had an alarming attraction to deception, subterfuge and living on the edge. Were he not a successful adman he might have been an effective spy.

Phil wasn't a cardplayer, but people often said he had a poker face. Unlike Julie, he'd always felt most comfortable keeping his feelings to himself, seldom showing much emotion, never crying, pretending all was well, hanging onto a superficial sense of order and structure at peril of giving into darker urges and tumbling into the abyss. The tight rein he held on himself was perceived by some as passivity, by his wife as a lack of spontaneity.

Julie was right, spontaneity wasn't his strong suit, even in bed. He was a knowledgeable lover, a skilled and considerate lover, sometimes even a passionate lover, but not a spontaneous one. He had done research in books and in the field to find out just where the clitoris and the G-spot were located. Every move he made was thought out in advance. Every move he made was designed to bring his partner, and then himself, to orgasm, and it was important to him that they both achieve it, preferably simultaneously. If they didn't he felt a failure. He kidded about it, and told Julie he was a Type A lover, but he wished that he were otherwise.

He had endless fantasies about Nanny, replaying the scene in her bedroom, with him yielding to her seductiveness. He savored the notion of being seduced, forced to do the things he craved without the responsibility. But in real life he had not succumbed to her, he had demanded that she change her behavior, and change it she had.

Yes, Nanny's behavior had changed, and so had Julie's. A certain calm had settled over Julie like a drop cloth. Perhaps even Harry noticed it, for he cried less and less lustily when Julie picked him up. Finally he let her pick him up without crying at all. Julie was starting to be happy again.

One evening, shortly after he'd come in from the office, Phil went into the kitchen to get a glass of orange juice. Nanny was washing lettuce at the sink.

"How are you tonight, Mr. Pressman?" said Nanny.

"Just fine, Nanny," said Phil, taking a white polyethylene container of juice out of the fridge.

"Did you have a good day at the office?" said Nanny.

"Not too bad, I guess," he said.

"Mr. Pressman, I have a confession to make to you," she said.

"Oh?" he said, filling up a glass and turning to look at her.

"Yes," she said. "Your advertising portfolio was lying out on the living-room coffee table this afternoon and I took the liberty of leafing through it. I hope that was all right?"

"Perfectly all right," said Phil, wondering where this was going.

"Did you write all of the adverts in that porfolio?" she said.

"Every one," he said, taking a sip of the cold juice.

"Well, I must tell you I'm impressed," said Nanny. "They are all so clever. I had no idea how clever you were."

"Why, thank you, Nanny," he said. "What a nice thing to say."

"I hope your employers pay you well," she said.

"Not well enough," he said.

She smiled at him and seemed to want to say more.

"Mr. Pressman . . ."

"Yes, Nanny?"

"I . . . want to thank you for being so understanding the other night and for . . . for not firing me," she said. "My behavior was unspeakable. You'd have been perfectly justified in insisting that I leave. I'm very grateful that you didn't."

"Well," said Phil, astonished at her candor, "thank you for telling me that."

"I have tried very hard to modify my behavior since that evening," she said. "I hope you've noticed the improvement."

"I have, indeed, Nanny," he said. "And I like it very much."

"If there is anything about me in the future that displeases you," she said, "I sincerely hope you won't hesitate to call it to my attention immediately. Will you do that for me?"

"I certainly will, Nanny," said Phil. "I certainly will."

CHAPTER 36

WHEN THE BRUSQUE WOMAN with the short gray hair entered the room, the man in the bed was gazing intently out the window at nothing in particular. The man's hair was as gray as the woman's, although he looked to be perhaps twenty years younger than she. More alarming was his skin, which was as gray as his hair. Framed by white sheets and pillows and the white wall at his back, the man was a study in monochrome.

The woman stood waiting for several moments for the man in the bed to acknowledge her before speaking, and when she did it was rather more deferential than one would have supposed from her general demeanor.

"Good evening, Mr. Parsons," she said.

The man in the bed did not immediately respond, but continued to gaze out the window at nothing in particular. After a while he turned and looked in her direction.

"Good evening, Miss Phipps," he said.

"How are you today, sir?" she said.

"Just fine," he said. "Couldn't possibly be better."

"I've brought the mail and the phone messages," she said, and carefully placed at the foot of the bed a packet of letters and a

77

collection of pink slips of paper with "While You Were Out" printed at the top of them.

"Thank you, Miss Phipps," he said, without evincing the slightest interest in the papers on the bed, and turned back to the window.

"Is there anything I can do for you?" she said.

"No no," he said. "They do everything for me here. It's quite wonderful."

"Is there anything you need?" she said.

The man did not reply. He continued to stare out the window.

"Anything at all?" she said.

"Nothing," he said at last. "I have everything I could possibly want here."

"Yes, sir," she said. "Well then, I expect I'll be going."

"Fine."

She hesitated a moment, waiting for something.

"I'll tell the gang at the office you said hello," she said finally.

"Oh, by all means," he said.

She turned toward the door before he could see that her eyes were watering.

CHAPTER 37

BECAUSE Harry no longer took Julie's breast, her milk dried up, she'd stopped nursing, and she was therefore able to start making excursions out of the apartment to the Design Center.

Julie's new clients were the Sharps from Teaneck, New Jersey. They had just bought a condo and were anxious to find a modular seating arrangement for the living room. Mr. Sharp, a short, delicate-looking, balding commodities broker with a skinny moustache and tinted aviator glasses, told Julie he was partial to contemporary—"preferably Postmodernist," he said. Mrs. Sharp, a petite, pinch-faced real estate broker with comically large horn-rimmed glasses, was partial to traditional—"preferably Early American," she said.

Julie shepherded them through a dozen wholesale showrooms in the Design Center, looking for Postmodernist Early American modular seating arrangements, in the course of which Mr. Sharp took Julie aside and confided that they were on a very tight budget, and Mrs. Sharp took Julie aside and confided that money was no object.

Julie tried to find them something relatively inexpensive in traditional, with very clean lines so it looked contemporary, but whatever she picked out for them was hated by either Mr. Sharp or Mrs. Sharp, except that sometimes it was hated by both.

Every so often one of them would like something and take the other off to the corner of the showroom where they would engage in angry whispers for several minutes. Then they would return to Julie with tight smiles on their faces, Mrs. Sharp would have tears in her eyes, and they would ask to go on to the next showroom.

After six hours of looking, Mr. and Mrs. Sharp were barely speaking to each other and Julie was rapidly developing another throbbing headache.

"I'll tell you what," said Julie. "Why don't you go to Macy's and Bloomingdale's and have a look around, and if you see any arrangements you like in either place, just write down the model numbers and I'll go back there and look at them with you."

"Didn't you want to come and counsel us?" said Mrs. Sharp disappointedly.

"Oh, I do," said Julie, "I really do. But I have a new baby at home and I have to get back and nurse him."

By the time she got home, the wet rawhide cords around Julie's forehead were so tight she could barely see straight. Nanny took one look at her and without a word led her right into the bedroom. There Nanny helped her off with her coat, shoes, skirt and blouse, put these swiftly into the closet and sat Julie down on the bed in her underwear.

As if caring for a small child, Nanny went swiftly into the bathroom, turned on the water in the tub and, without consulting Julie, came back to finish the undressing. Nanny took off Julie's pantyhose, removed her bra, placed her firmly face down on the bed in her panties, and began to work on her back and shoulders.

"Difficult day?" said Nanny.

"The worst," said Julie. "The *worst*."

"You can tell me about it if you like," said Nanny.

Grateful for the opportunity to let some of it out, Julie began describing Mr. and Mrs. Sharp, their conflicting desires for Postmodernist and Early American furniture and their abominable taste.

Nanny chuckled as she kneaded and pummeled Julie's back, and Julie, with Nanny's encouragement, was inspired to greater and greater heights of wicked parody in describing her clients.

"Didn't you want to come and *coun*-sel us?" said Julie, in petulant parody of Mrs. Sharp.

Julie decided that Mr. Sharp looked like a bald eagle and Mrs. Sharp like an owl. By the time the bathtub was full, both women were shrieking with laughter at the eagle and the owl.

Nanny helped Julie into the bathroom, poured some bubble bath into the tub, slipped off Julie's panties and settled her into the suds. Because Nanny was a nurse and because she had been so matter-of-fact about the whole procedure, Julie had no more than fleeting reservations about the appropriateness of letting her employee undress her.

"You know," said Julie happily, as Nanny shampooed her hair,

"I wasn't at all comfortable with you when you first came to live with us."

"That's not surprising," said Nanny, working the lather into Julie's scalp. "I wasn't comfortable with you either."

"You weren't?" said Julie. "Really?"

"Heavens no," said Nanny. "I daresay you and your husband have quite a different approach to servants than I've been used to."

"I suppose so," said Julie.

"You especially, Mrs. Pressman," said Nanny, tilting Julie's head back to rinse her hair under the hand sprayer. "You seemed to want to be my peer, and that made me uncomfortable. At least at first—classical nanny training in the U.K. and all that. Now I must say I rather like it."

"Really?" said Julie.

"Yes," said Nanny. "I almost feel as though we're school chums."

"Me too," said Julie. "Isn't that remarkable."

"And yet I also feel oddly maternal toward you," said Nanny, soaping Julie's back and shoulders with a large sponge, "even though I expect we are scarcely five years apart in age. I do believe you need a lot of mothering."

"Mmmmm," said Julie. "I guess you're right."

"And I'm delighted to provide that for you," said Nanny, soaping Julie's arms and underarms and breasts.

"Did you have a good relationship with your mother when you were a little girl?" said Nanny.

Julie considered a moment before replying.

"Yes and no," said Julie. "I mean I always thought that Mom and I were very close when I was little—I have lots of memories of her teaching me how to sew, how to cook, and stuff like that. But I also know now that she was overwhelmed by motherhood, and I must have sensed that somehow even then. I mean I must have sensed that, deep down inside, she was too weak to really give me the mothering I needed. So I had to grow up a lot faster

81

than I wanted to, and from the time I was ten I was more a mother to my mother than she was to me. Does that make any sense?"

"Perfect sense," said Nanny.

"What was *your* mother like?" said Julie.

Nanny's face grew brittle for a moment and then relaxed.

"Both of my parents were absolutely ghastly," said Nanny.

"Oh, I'm sorry," said Julie.

"I, too, had no childhood," said Nanny.

"Maybe that's why you're such a good nanny now," said Julie.

"Maybe so," said Nanny.

When Nanny had finished with the bath, she helped Julie out of the tub and briskly dried her off with a huge bath sheet.

"Nanny," said Julie tentatively, "I wonder if I could ask you some medical advice about something rather . . . intimate?"

"Of course, dear," said Nanny, helping Julie on with her night-gown. "What is it you wish to know?"

"Well," said Julie, "my obstetrician told me that my episiotomy would be fully healed six weeks after delivery and I could begin having sex again . . ."

"Yes . . ."

"But it's been that long and sex is just . . . too painful. Is that normal?"

"Perfectly normal, dear," said Nanny, beginning to blow-dry Julie's hair and to brush it out with long strokes.

"I just feel so bad about depriving Phil," she said.

"Don't worry about Mr. Pressman," said Nanny. "Worry about yourself. Mr. Pressman will be just fine."

CHAPTER 38

ALTHOUGH he stopped by Sullivan's office three more times, her secretary was oddly unable to give Phil any indication of when he might have an audience with the busy agency president. First, a surprise crisis had come up on the campaign for some automotive account they were pitching. Then Sullivan was working at home and couldn't be disturbed. Then an out-of-town client had come in unexpectedly and needed to be entertained.

Phil was beginning to feel he was getting the runaround. He was surprised and disappointed. From all he had heard about Mary Margaret Sullivan, he'd expected better from her than that. If she'd simply called him into her office and said, Look, in the old days I was an idealist and I refused to take on products that I thought were bad, but I no longer have that luxury anymore and I've had to make compromises, so you can move to another account if it bothers you—that, at least he could deal with.

That, at least, would take a little courage on her part. But to keep putting him off and not even deal with him directly—that, he felt, was really shabby. That, he felt, was inexcusable. Perhaps, if she continued to avoid him, he would have to force her to talk to him.

Although Julie's episiotomy had finally healed, sex was still too painful to be considered seriously, so she and Phil had to content themselves with unfulfilling sessions of cuddling in bed.

The proximity of Nanny and the memory of her attempt at seducing him had caused Phil's horniness to compress into a gem-like hardness capable of scratching glass.

One morning Phil was awakened shortly before 6 a.m. by the

83

sound of Nanny feeding Harry in the kitchen. Though Julie stirred and groaned, she succeeded in remaining asleep.

Phil was not so fortunate. At length he arose, went into the bathroom to urinate, then wandered into the kitchen for a cup of coffee. The sight which greeted Phil in the kitchen caused him to suspect he was still asleep.

Nanny was seated in the white wicker rocking chair with Harry in her arms. The top of Nanny's uniform appeared to be open. It looked to Phil as though the baby were sucking at her breast.

"What are you *doing?*" said Phil.

Nanny smiled at Phil, shifted Harry to a new position in her arms, and Phil was no longer certain of what he had seen.

CHAPTER 39

JULIE was reluctant to wake up. Phil continued to shake her shoulder.

"Please . . . " she whispered, still trying to cling to the last shreds of sleep, "jus' lemme have another hour . . ."

"Julie," said Phil, "Nanny was nursing the baby."

Julie groaned.

"Another hour . . ."

"Julie, Nanny was breast-feeding your son."

Julie opened her eyes.

"I just walked in on them in the kitchen," said Phil. "I thought I was dreaming."

Julie picked her head up from her bashed-in pillow. Her eyes were focusing with difficulty.

"What are you saying?" she said.

"I think you heard me," said Phil.

Julie shook her head, then let it sink back down on the pillow and closed her eyes.

"You were dreaming," she said.

"You don't believe me?" said Phil.

Julie sighed.

"That Nanny had milk in her breasts and was suckling our son? No, Phil, I don't."

"Julie, I saw it with my own eyes."

"It's impossible, Phil. It's a physiological impossibility."

"I read in our breast-feeding book about an adoptive mother who was eventually able to produce milk by means of hormones and massage," said Phil.

Julie's face tried on several emotions in rapid order, as if searching for one which might fit.

"Don't do this to me, Phil," she said quietly. "Please don't do this to me."

"Don't do *what* to you?"

A smile flickered briefly. It didn't fit and it faded. Tears slipped down her cheeks.

"Things with Nanny were just starting to get better," said Julie. "Please don't spoil it, baby. Please."

Phil considered this. His wife was telling him that she didn't want to know anything bad about the nanny. His wife was telling him that she couldn't survive without the nanny. It was the first time in a long while that she had called him baby.

"O.K., kid," said Phil. "Whatever you say."

CHAPTER 40

PHIL had come to a decision. He would go along with Julie's expressed desire to know no more bad things about Nanny, at least for a while. People who loved each other could at least do that—tell each other the lies they wanted to hear, spare them the truths they found too painful to hear.

And perhaps Julie was right. Perhaps, despite Nanny's bizarre behavior, they really couldn't get along without her. Perhaps Nanny's taking baths with the baby and trying to wet-nurse him—assuming the latter had really happened—weren't really doing him any harm. Logically speaking, it shouldn't be any more harmful for Nanny to take baths with the baby and nurse him than it was for Julie. Despite Phil's earnest assurances to Julie to the contrary, the baby probably wouldn't even know the difference. Perhaps there *wasn't* a difference.

Perhaps. Perhaps Nanny *hadn't* been nursing the baby. Perhaps he had hallucinated that. It wouldn't have been totally impossible to have hallucinated such a thing, given the stress he'd been under the past few weeks. It wouldn't have been totally impossible. And he was, after all, an acknowledged paranoid.

Julie had definitely made some sort of peace with Nanny. In fact, they suddenly seemed as close as schoolgirls. It was, he thought, not really so surprising. The oppressed identifying with their oppressors was a common psychological phenomenon. Inmates of prisons often emulated their guards, kidnap victims their abductors. Patty Hearst became a machine-gun–toting soldier in the Symbionese Liberation Army. A throwback to when we were all prisoners of our parents. Maybe that's what was happening between Julie and Nanny. Maybe that's why she was willing to turn a blind eye to whatever Nanny might or might not have been doing.

Phil hoped that was it, because another possibility had suggested itself to him, one he wasn't anxious to pursue. The possibility that Nanny had been as seductive with Julie as she had with him. The possibility that Julie had succumbed to Nanny, become her lover.

No, that wasn't possible. Julie didn't have a thing for women, of that Phil was certain. He would've seen some evidence of it in the past if she did, and he never had. Still, anything was possible. Nothing Nanny did would surprise him, including trying to seduce his wife. Phil tried to imagine Julie and Nanny lying in bed together in one another's arms, stroking each other's hair, kissing, bare flesh pressed against bare flesh, and he shuddered.

CHAPTER 41

"Ms. SULLIVAN *is* in," said her secretary, "but she's busy."

"Doing what?" said Phil.

"Excuse me?"

"What is she doing?" said Phil.

"Working," said the secretary.

"Tell her I want to see her," he said.

"She *knows* you want to see her."

"Tell her I want to see her *now*."

The secretary glared at him.

"Ms. Sullivan is busy *working*," said the secretary with clenched jaws. "She will see you when she has a moment free."

Phil strode up to Sullivan's office door and opened it.

"What are you *doing?*" said the secretary, shocked.

"Don't worry about it," said Phil, stepping into Sullivan's office.

87

Mary Margaret Sullivan looked up, genuinely startled.

"What are you doing in here?" she said.

"I'm sorry to be barging in on you like this, Ms. Sullivan," said Phil, beginning to suspect this was a horrid mistake, "but I have a serious problem and it's imperative that I speak to you immediately,"

"Are you so insensitive that you can't tell when someone is busy?" she said, fuming.

Phil's face got hot with embarrassment. This was truly the worst thing he had ever done in advertising and it would probably get him fired, but he felt too strongly about the notion of convincing people to drink coffee that would give them cancer to contain his outrage any longer.

"Are you so insensitive that you can't tell when your company is recklessly endangering people's lives?" said Phil.

Sullivan's face was bright with rage.

"What in the *devil* are you talking about?" she said.

"What I'm talking about," said Phil, beginning to speak quietly and rapidly, trying not to leave any holes between words through which she could interrupt, "is that you are paying me to compose ads which will persuade innocent people to buy and drink a coffee which—because it's decaffeinated by means of a process utilizing a chemical called methylene chloride which has produced cancer in laboratory animals rather than by means of the Swiss water process or by means of a chemical called ethyl acetate, which is a safe, naturally occurring compound approved by the F.D.A. and utilized by—"

"*Hold* it!" said Sullivan, and Phil stopped. "Who told you Java is decaffeinated with methylene chloride?"

"Uh, Ralph Roberts did," said Phil.

"Ralph Roberts told you Java is decaffeinated with methylene chloride?"

"Well," said Phil, "not in so many words, perhaps, but he did say—"

"If Ralph told you that he's lying," said Sullivan. "Java is de-caffeinated with ethyl acetate, just like High Point and Folger's."

Phil stared at her.

"It is?" he said stupidly.

"Yes."

"Uh, are you sure?" said Phil, beginning to perspire quite freely.

"Absolutely sure," she said. "That's one of the first things I asked them when we took the account."

"I see," said Phil, taking out his handkerchief and beginning to mop his now streaming face and neck. "I'm afraid I owe you an apology. I guess I got a little carried away there and—"

"A *little* carried away?" said Sullivan.

"It's just that I happen to know a little about decaffeinated coffee because of my wife's recent pregnancy and—"

"And a little knowledge *is* a dangerous thing," she said.

"—and when I asked Ralph Roberts what they used to decaf-feinate Java, all he'd say was not to worry about it. I honestly thought he was covering up the fact that it was done with methy-lene chloride. And then when I couldn't get in to see you, I thought *you* were putting me off, too."

Sullivan shook her head in pity.

"Well, I've made a damned fool of myself," said Phil miserably, "and I wouldn't blame you at all if you wanted to fire me for this."

Sullivan looked at him for several moments and then chuckled fondly.

"You *have* made a damned fool of yourself," she said, "but I don't want to fire you. I've been following your work here very closely, Pressman, and I've been very impressed. I need people with ability like yours."

"Thank you," he said.

"But I really must tell you," she said, chuckling again, "that I haven't seen such rampant paranoia in many a year."

"I'm sorry," said Phil. "I don't know what more I can say."

"I should also say I haven't seen such a strong moral stance taken in this business in many a year either," she said. "As misguided as it was, it took a lot of moxie for you to come bursting in here the way you did."

"It did?" said Phil.

She nodded.

"Say, how's that baby of yours?" she said.

"Oh, better," said Phil, relieved to be talking about anything else. "Much better."

"Did you hire a nurse as I told you?"

"Yes."

"Good. O.K., Pressman, you'd better let me get back to work here."

"O.K."

She smiled up at him.

"I'll sleep better at night now," she said with a wink, "knowing that Phil Pressman is patrolling the agency's moral code."

Phil gave her a bland smile and a diffident wave and headed for the door.

"Pressman?"

"Yes?"

"Anytime you want to talk about anything," she said warmly, "I promise I'll listen. You don't have to break down the door."

"Thank you, Ms. Sullivan."

CHAPTER 42

THE SHARPS had found a seating arrangement in Bloomingdale's that they neither loved nor loathed but thought they could live with, and insisted that Julie meet them there when the store opened. She got up and left the apartment just as Phil went into the bathroom for his morning shower.

Phil turned on the hot water, took off his shorts and T-shirt, and when the shower had filled the stall with fog, stepped into it. He savored the needles of hot water on his upper back and neck and began to soap himself. He thought he heard the bathroom door open and assumed Julie had forgotten something and returned.

It wasn't Julie. Through the steamed glass of the shower door Phil could make out a ghostly white presence in the room—Nanny in her starched white uniform. Phil's heart began to race. What in the name of God . . .

"What are you doing?" he said.

Nanny moved slowly toward the shower stall. Taking her time, taking her own sweet time, taking all the time in the world, Nanny reached for the aluminum handle of the shower door and slid it open.

"Get out of here," he said.

Nanny's face wore a bemused expression.

"You need to be more spontaneous, Mr. Pressman," she said. "You need to be in the moment more. Isn't that what Mrs. Pressman is always telling you?"

She stared quite frankly at Phil's body, focusing particular attention on his soaped-up crotch. He felt vulnerable, angry, aroused, confused. What could she possibly . . .

"Get out of here *now*," he said.

Nanny slowly untied and removed each of her white leather shoes, then stepped into the shower, fully clothed, and pulled the sliding door shut. The hot water from the shower head splattered her uniform, diluting its opacity, gluing it to her skin. Every garment of hers and the section of body it encased was as visible to Phil as if he had suddenly been empowered with X-ray vision.

The same trancelike dizziness that overcame him in her bedroom the night he tried to fire her was overcoming him now.

"Relax, Mr. Pressman," she said. "Be in the moment. Be here now, as they used to say in the sixties."

She floated toward him without having taken another step. He backed away, but there was nowhere to go. He stood facing her, his back against the shower stall wall, unwilling for this to continue, unable to stop it.

"Please go," he whispered.

She slid her arms around his neck and pressed her body up against his. He was aware of the sensation of the drenched cloth of her uniform against his bare flesh. He felt himself grow hard. He had never asked for this. He had tried to fend it off before. It couldn't possibly be his responsibility any longer. It might not even be happening.

She pressed her lips to his forehead, his cheek, his neck, his lips. He stood still and let it happen. Maybe Julie was right. Being in the moment didn't seem so bad at that. Nanny slid a cool tongue between his teeth, found the tip of his tongue with her own. She sucked his tongue into her mouth and bit it. He whimpered involuntarily.

He tentatively put his arms around her neck, and she withdrew. Smiling, she opened the shower door and backed out of the stall, creating an instant lake on the tiled floor. She grabbed his bath towel, wrapped it around her streaming hair, then left the room. It took him awhile to become disengorged.

Living in the same apartment with Nanny was like careless smoking in a warehouse full of dynamite. Phil was wound up so tight he was ready to snap. He resented Nanny's sexual teasing, but realized he found it too exciting to fire her. Besides, because of Nanny, Julie was happy again—Harry was once more responding to her and he no longer cried when she picked him up.

Yesterday Phil had come upon a wonderful scene, Julie playing with Harry in the kitchen. Julie was seated in the rocking chair and Harry was lying on her knees, facing her. Harry put his arms over his head. Julie put her arms over her head. Harry broke into a wonderful toothless grin. Then he dropped his arms and raised them over his head again. Julie mimicked him and he seemed to find that hilarious. They kept raising their arms over their heads and lowering them, and Harry laughed out loud.

The sound of Harry's laughter had made Phil teary. That sort of scene had been possible because of Nanny. It was worth everything to Julie. What was it worth to Phil?

CHAPTER 43

WHEN JULIE ARRIVED at Bloomingdale's the Sharps informed her that they had had a change of heart.

"Neither of us really liked it," said Mrs. Sharp, "and we figured at these prices, why compromise?"

Julie got back to the apartment just as Phil was leaving for work. She couldn't believe what she was seeing on the floor.

"My *God*, Phil," she said, "look at all this water on the carpet!"

"I was in the shower and I thought I heard the phone," he said.

"You tracked water all through the bedroom and the living room and the hallway to the other bedrooms," she said.

"I'm sorry, Julie," he said. "I didn't realize I was dripping that much."

Julie regarded her husband carefully.

"The phone is right here in the bedroom," she said. "How come there are wet footprints all the way to the back bedrooms? To Nanny's bedroom?"

"How come?" he said. "I'll tell you how come. Because once I got into the bedroom and picked up the phone—it was a wrong number, by the way—I thought I heard Harry crying. I don't seem

93

to be able to soothe him anymore, so I went to look for Nanny."

"I see," she said. "Well then, I suppose that explains it."

It didn't, though, she thought. There was something odd about the story. There was something odd about the way Phil had told it. Phil was very odd of late, in fact. She wondered what was going on with him. She wondered if he had the hots for Nanny. She hoped there wasn't going to be a repetition of the time at the U. of I. when his childish fooling around with other women had nearly forced her to give him up.

Phil was, at times, very childish indeed. Sometimes she wasn't sure he knew he was Harry's father. Sometimes she wasn't sure he knew he was Julie's husband.

He had periods of varying length when for no particular reason he stopped doing the things he usually did around the house, when he allowed Julie to pick up after him, to put away his dirty socks and underwear, when he stopped knowing where anything was and had to get Julie to find it, when he seemed to expect approval for the sorts of things Julie herself did without question, like making the bed, as if for her making the bed was expected but with him it was a special favor that he was doing her. In those times he seemed to her more like her son than her husband.

He never seemed to enjoy these periods very much, but he lapsed into them anyway. It had to be very tempting for a man to allow the woman he lived with to take care of him, she thought. It was such a familiar feeling, like when he was a little boy and his mom did everything for him. Unfortunately, when the man was grown up and when the woman he lived with was his wife, it didn't work. Turning your wife into your mother wasn't satisfying for either party, and it absolutely killed romance.

Not that poor Phil had a choice in that area now, she thought. So long as sex continued to be painful for her she wasn't going to be very available to him. Phil had suggested they try to satisfy each other orally, but she hadn't been responsive to the idea, although she'd liked it well enough before the baby came. She didn't know why the idea of oral sex no longer appealed to her. It just didn't

94

seem to be appropriate to her anymore. Perhaps it was because she was now a mother.

Every time she looked at Harry she marveled at the fact of his creation and thought of how Phil's blood and tissue and hers were united within him. It was a powerful emotional concept. It made her and Phil truly family, truly blood relatives. It somehow didn't seem quite right for blood relatives to have sex with each other.

She realized what a strain total abstinence must be putting on Phil. She realized that if she continued to be unavailable to him she would eventually force him to look elsewhere for satisfaction. She wondered if that were happening already. She wondered if her reluctance to have sex with Phil was more psychological than physical.

Maybe she, like Phil, was behaving in a less than grownup fashion. Allowing Nanny to take over the household like an all-powerful mother had certainly caused Julie to feel like a little girl again—like Harry's older sister instead of Harry's mother.

Maybe the peace she'd made with Nanny—pleasant though it was to be so totally and lovingly taken care of—was actually her own version of Phil's behaving like a boy. She would have to think about that one. Or *not* think about it, which might be easier.

CHAPTER 44

THE NURSE was encouraged. Mr. Parsons had for the first time since his arrival on her ward asked for a wastebasket and actually appeared to be interested in his mail.

Indeed, when the wastebasket was brought into his room, he

spread approximately two hundred letters out over the surface of the bed and looked at them with more interest than she remembered seeing on his face since his arrival, shortly after the tragedy.

"Feeling better today, huh, Mr. Parsons?"

"Oh, marvelous," he said. "Tip-top."

"I'm so glad," she said. "Well, have fun now."

"Oh, I will."

When she had gone, Parsons carefully arranged all the unopened letters according to size. The smallest ones went in the front, the largest in the back. Then he spread out the pink phone messages.

Working quickly and surely, he folded the first three pink slips into impressive origami versions of a pelican, a rabbit and an armadillo. Next he opened the twelve smallest envelopes and inserted a pink slip in each one before depositing them soberly in the wastebasket.

Another nurse came in, saw what he was doing and smiled.

"Oh, you're *working*," she said delightedly.

"Yes."

"Just look at all those letters and phone messages," she said. "I wouldn't even know where to start."

Parsons managed a polite smile.

"I hardly know myself," he said.

"Oh-oh," she said. "Here's one that got away."

She picked up a pink slip that had drifted under the bed and handed it to him.

"Thank you," he said.

"Not at all. You just ring if there's anything you need, all right?"

"Absolutely."

The nurse turned and left the room.

Parsons continued to hold the pink slip the nurse had given him for several minutes after she had gone. This one, he noted, had lots of typing on it. If he folded it type-side out, it might make an interesting all-over pattern. He wondered what shape he ought to fold it in. He finally decided upon a kangaroo.

As he was making the first fold, a name on the message caught his eye. The name was Luci Redman.

Luci Redman.

Holding the pink slip of paper, his hand began to shake. He'd gone to such elaborate lengths to separate himself from his old life and from anything that might remind him of what happened to him and to his family. And yet here was that accursed name again, right in this room where he'd imagined he was safe, right on this piece of paper which he held in his hand.

He opened the pink piece of paper and smoothed it flat and looked carefully at the message, and a muffled roaring began sounding in his ears. The message was from a Mr. Pressman. There was a New York phone number.

The roaring in his ears grew louder. He crumpled up the message and threw it into the wastebasket.

CHAPTER 45

NANNY'S DAY OFF. Phil dressed Harry in his snowsuit and took him downstairs for a walk in the stroller. Unsavory-looking street people in bizarre outfits, some wearing capes of filthy plastic bubble-wrap, muttering silently or conducting full-blown animated dialogues with themselves, passed them on the relatively deserted residential street.

Phil wondered if any of them were dangerous. Crazed street people in New York sometimes attacked pedestrians without warning. He wondered how he'd protect his baby if one of them suddenly went berserk. Perhaps the busier thoroughfares were safer. Phil pushed the stroller toward Twelfth Avenue.

Cars and tractor-trailers thundered past them on Twelfth Avenue and Phil felt momentarily reassured by the noise and motion. Then he recalled news stories of cabs running red lights, smashing into other cars, ricocheting up onto curbs, pinning people against lampposts and mailboxes, squooshing them till red jelly squirted out of them like squeezed jelly doughnuts.

His little son seemed so vulnerable in his stroller. If anything ever happened to Harry, Phil wondered if he could take it. Julie couldn't, he felt sure. She'd sink into despair and probably have to be sent to a sanitarium.

Phil picked Harry up out of the stroller and carried him in his arms, nudging the stroller along with his body, and headed back toward their apartment.

At home Phil undressed Harry and changed his poopy diaper, wondering where babies who drink only liquids get solid poop. Then, while Julie tried to nurse him, Phil filled up the tub for Harry's bath.

Shortly after setting the baby down in the tub, marveling at how well he was holding his head up without flopping over, Phil sneezed. Harry burst into terrified tears. No matter what he did, Phil was unable to console him, and the bath ended with Harry still screaming.

"Your sneeze scared him, that's all," said Julie. "He's just a little baby."

"I know that," said Phil.

"You seem mad at him for crying," said Julie.

"Not at all," said Phil.

"Then why are you sulking?"

"I'm not sulking," said Phil, but he knew he was.

"Hey," said Julie.

She whipped out her breast and squirted milk in Phil's face. At first he was startled, then he touched the tip of his tongue to the droplets near his mouth and found them sweet and malty-tasting.

"What would you say to taking a bath with me after the kid goes to bed?" he said.

Julie smiled coyly.

"Candles and wine come with it?"

"Absolutely."

"You got it."

When Harry finally fell asleep, they ringed the tub with votive candles, filled it with bubble bath, opened a bottle of wine and got in. Phil worried about Julie drinking while she was still nursing, but Julie had found permission in a book on nursing, and Phil relaxed.

Both of them were beginning to feel mellow after only a single glass of wine, and then Harry began to cry. At first they both pretended not to hear it. Then they both sighed, got out of the tub, put on robes and went to see what the trouble was. When Harry was quiet again they returned to the tub, but the bubbles had dissipated, and with them their playful mood.

They got ready for bed and Phil suggested they try making love, but Julie wasn't eager to get through the pain, so they just got under the covers and turned their backs and composed themselves for sleep.

CHAPTER 46

LATE THAT NIGHT Phil and Julie lay asleep in their room. Julie snored to Phil's right, hugging her pillow, a safe proxy for a painful husband.

In his sleep Phil heard the soft sound of their bedroom door being opened and closed. Had somebody come into the room? If he'd been awake, he would have known.

Several layers below consciousness, Phil heard a floorboard creak under the carpeting, felt a presence materialize at his side of the bed, heard it sink to the carpeting with an audible snapping of leg muscles and tendons, sensed a hand being inserted under the covers on his side of the bed, snaking over the smooth sheets until it touched warm flesh.

He swam upward through layers of awareness, imagined the hand fingerwalking along the mattress, along his chest, down his chest to his waist, then across his waist to his left thigh. He broke the surface of wakefulness and felt the hand walk down his left thigh to the outside of his left leg to his foot, then across the sole of his left foot and up the inside of his left leg to his thigh again.

Was he still asleep, and this just one of those dreams where you kept dreaming you're awakening while remaining asleep?

Now the hand lightly brushed the crotch of his jockey shorts. Now it passed over his crotch to his opposite thigh. Now it returned to his crotch.

Phil held his breath, not daring to make a sound. He remained absolutely motionless.

Now a second hand slid under the covers and snaked over the sheets. Now he felt his jockey shorts being tugged ever so gently downward, down over his hips to his thighs, releasing his penis.

Julie continued to snore softly to his right, oblivious to the perversity of what was happening inches away from her.

Now a head followed the two hands under the covers, a mole burrowing under turf, and now two lips were caressing the end of his member. Now the lips drew the tip slowly into a warm wet place.

Phil suppressed a groan of excruciating pleasure. Suddenly, as suddenly as they'd appeared, lips, head and hands withdrew from under the covers. There was another creak of the floorboards, and then another. The door softly opened and closed.

Bursting with frustration, Phil moved against Julie's warm body in the bed. She shifted in her sleep, groaned, turned over and moved slightly away from him.

Phil pulled his shorts back up and tried to compose himself for sleep. Sleep was no longer a possibility. He lay there awake, imagining the conclusion of what Nanny had started.

CHAPTER 47

IT HAD BECOME important to Phil to find out more about Nanny. To see what other people's experience of her had been, to know the dimensions of her perversity, to gauge the damage she might do if allowed to remain.

Phil took out Nanny's résumé and looked it over. It seemed legitimate. It listed two impressive-sounding schools in England, some university-level work at Trinity College in Dublin, a full term in a nursing school and a few years spent as a staff nurse at the St. Barnabas Hospital in London.

Phil picked up the telephone, got Overseas Information and obtained a phone number for St. Barnabas. Then he placed a call to the hospital and requested the Records Department. But the first woman he talked to thought he wanted patient information, and the second thought he wanted information on current staff, and by the time he got the person in the department he wanted he was afraid that Nanny was going to return any minute, and besides, he was beginning to worry about how much the call was costing, so he was reluctant to spend much time with her.

The woman made a quick check of the records and didn't find any Luci Redman as a recent employee of the hospital, but Phil specified the years that Luci Redman purported to have worked there and suggested that the woman call back collect if she found anything at all. He gave her both his work and home numbers.

He placed another call to Conroy, the Houston oilman, and the secretary seemed piqued to be hearing from him again.

"I have given Mr. Conroy your message, Mr. Pressman," she said, "and that is all that I can do."

"I understand," said Phil. "Perhaps you could just tell him of the urgency of my need to speak with him."

"If you have already employed this individual," said the secretary, "I fail to see why you need to speak with him about her."

"Please just tell him of my request," said Phil.

"Very well," she said.

Phil phoned Parsons, the investment banker in Detroit.

"I have given Mr. Parsons your message, Mr. Pressman," said Parsons's secretary, also piqued. "I am sure that he will call you when he is able."

"Do you think it will be soon?" said Phil.

"I would not presume to speculate on when it might be," said the secretary.

"I see," said Phil. "You know, I think I might be able to appreciate Mr. Parsons's current situation a little better if you could give me some idea of the nature of the tragedy that he suffered."

At first there was no reply. Then:

"I do not know what sort of secretaries you are accustomed to dealing with, Mr. Pressman," she said frostily, "but I would no more discuss my employer's personal business with a complete stranger than I would fly to the moon."

And with that she cut him off.

CHAPTER 48

NANNY had taken Harry for a walk. Phil quietly slipped into her room to have a look around. He didn't quite know what he was looking for. A few sheets of his and Julie's stationery would have been a start.

Nanny's bed was neatly made with hospital corners. The blankets were so tight you could have bounced a quarter on them. He went to the chest of drawers, and trying to replace things in the precise positions in which he found them, he began to go through the contents.

There were bras, panties, pantyhose and slips, mostly in white. There were also a few red bras and panties, and a few black ones. There were a black garter belt and black nylon stockings. There were blouses, belts, sweaters, socks, silk scarves, lace hankies and two surprisingly dowdy swimsuits.

Going through somebody's personal effects without their knowledge was titillating. It quickened Phil's pulse beyond the simple prospect of being caught.

In the bottom drawer there were a small antique jewelry case and an ancient folder for keeping personal documents and important letters. Phil was just about to open the jewelry case when he thought he heard a noise at the other end of the apartment. He swiftly closed the drawers and went to the bedroom door.

"Hello?" he called out tentatively.

There was no response.

"Julie?" he called.

Still no reply.

"Nanny?"

Nothing. There were no further noises from the other end of the apartment. If Nanny had come back, he would surely have heard her or the baby by now.

103

Inside Nanny's jewelry case were several pairs of antique earrings for pierced ears, an elegant antique watch, several gold bracelets, several antique gold neck chains, a small gold crucifix and two surprisingly expensive-looking diamond rings. If the diamonds were real, he thought, they had no business being in a chest of drawers. He didn't know what diamonds went for, but these looked as if they might be worth quite a lot of money.

He opened the document file and looked quickly through the contents. There were several old letters, so old they appeared to be crumbling with the slow fire that attacks paper over the years. There were some photocopies of legal documents relating to the nursing profession. There was a passport and a visa and a green working card for foreigners.

Phil looked at the photo in Nanny's passport. The photo bore a fairly close resemblance to Nanny, but the paper on which it was printed seemed older than he'd expected. He checked the date on the passport and was amazed to see that it had expired at least twelve years before.

Phil went next to the closet and looked through the clothes hanging from the bar. Encased in polyethylene bags, there were two white uniforms, a silk nightgown, a silk bathrobe and a checkered flannel shirt.

Phil looked along the floor and sorted through pairs of sensible white nurse's shoes, Reebok running shoes, and then he found a small purse with a lock on it. He tried to release the catch, but it was clear this purse could be opened only with a key.

He went to the chest of drawers and found a hairpin and came back to the purse and tried to pick the lock. He didn't really know what he was doing, but he'd seen it done so often on TV and in the movies he figured it was worth a try.

He fiddled with the hairpin for several minutes and now he definitely heard someone at the front door. He quickly put the purse back in the bottom of the closet, crept to the door of the bedroom and carefully let himself out into the hall, just as Nanny entered with the baby.

CHAPTER 49

PARSONS lay on his stark white bed in his stark white room and stared at the stark white ceiling and cursed Mr. Pressman in New York who had had the effrontery to invade the small world he had so meticulously constructed to insulate himself from his previous life.

Parsons turned his gaze from the ceiling to the white telephone on the small white stand by his bed. He stared at it for several minutes, at the rows of thin rectangular buttons, at the tightly coiled flat cord leading into the receiver, at the thick round cord leading into the wall. And then, cursing, he reached into the wastebasket and took out the crumpled piece of pink paper and smoothed it out, picked up the receiver and signaled the operator, and placed the person-to-person call to New York.

CHAPTER 50

"SIT DOWN, sit down, take a load off," said Ralph Roberts.

Phil seated himself before Roberts's impossibly cluttered desk.

"How's the wife and kid?"

"Great," said Phil. "Couldn't be better."

"And how's that nanny of yours?"

A huge wink from Roberts.

"Great too," said Phil, ignoring the wink.

"Still humping her brains out?" said Roberts.

"Every night," said Phil.

Roberts chuckled.

"Reason I called you in here, Phil, is we're giving you that bonus for thinking up the name for Java after all. Actually, Sullivan insisted you deserve it."

"That's great," said Phil happily.

"Should help buy baby new shoes, eh?" said Roberts.

"You can say that again," said Phil.

"And perhaps a trinket or two for that long-legged nanny of yours," said Roberts.

"Oh, absolutely," said Phil.

Roberts chuckled.

"You're not fooling anybody, you know."

"What?" said Phil.

"You think if you *agree* you're humping her and you're that casual about it, you'll convince me you're *not* humping her," said Roberts. "But it's too casual. I can tell you're as far into her skivvies as you could get without wearing them."

"You can tell that, can you?" said Phil.

"It's all right, I don't fault you for being discreet," said Roberts.

Phil studied Roberts's grizzled, mischievous face a moment and wondered what it would be like to trust him. Phil didn't have a shrink or a priest or a friend he could talk to about it, and he certainly couldn't confide in his wife. It would be a relief to be able to talk to somebody.

"What if I told you," said Phil, "what's really going on with our nanny?"

CHAPTER 51

JULIE was sitting on the toilet, looking over a catalogue of bath-room fixtures, when the telephone rang. Nanny was attending to Harry in the kitchen and Julie assumed Nanny would answer it.

The phone continued to ring.

In the kitchen Nanny finally answered.

"Pressman residence," she said.

"I have a person-to-person call for Mr. Pressman," said a long-distance operator.

"Who is calling?" said Nanny.

"What is your name, sir?" said the operator.

There was silence from the other end.

"Sir?" said the operator.

Then the line went dead.

"He seems to have hung up, hon," said the operator. "Well, it takes all kinds."

"It certainly does," said Nanny and hung up.

"Who was that, Nanny?" said Julie, coming into the kitchen.

"Wrong number," said Nanny.

Parsons had difficulty replacing the receiver in its cradle because of how badly his hand was shaking. The moment he'd heard Luci Redman's voice he'd hung up, but it was too late. The images began flooding back into his brain, the images he had so carefully locked away, and he began to sob.

CHAPTER 52

NANNY had taken Harry out to the market to buy groceries. Phil went back into her bedroom to his sneaky work.

He took a hairpin out of her chest of drawers, went back into her closet and located the locked purse. After several minutes of poking about inside the lock with the hairpin, he heard the tiniest of clicks and the catch released. He opened the purse and looked inside.

He had expected to find thousands of dollars in large bills or perhaps more jewelry. There were scarcely more than two hundred dollars in American money, some British bank notes, a checkbook, a case of traveler's checks, some keys, some makeup and a small antique gold locket in the shape of a heart.

There were also some curious things. Two candles burned about halfway through. A tiny little leather pouch filled with what looked like incense, another filled with what looked like seeds and a third with what appeared to be sand.

He picked up the antique gold locket and released the catch, peered at the photo inside of it and gasped. The photo was the very last thing he ever expected to see inside of any locket belonging to Luci Redman.

The photo was a tiny picture of himself, Julie and the baby.

CHAPTER 53

PHIL was at first rather moved. The idea that Nanny would have a photo of him and Julie and the baby in a little heart-shaped gold locket, hidden away inside her purse in the bottom of her closet —as if to guarantee that no one would ever discover she had any tender feelings for the family for whom she worked—opened up another set of possibilities which gave her a dimension and a texture that he could not help finding attractive.

Perhaps, he thought, Nanny wasn't what she seemed. Perhaps she was a warm and tender person at heart, so bruised and toughened by God only knew what circumstances of upbringing in England that she had to cover up the softness, the vulnerability, lest it destroy her. Perhaps, just as he'd suggested to Julie the night he tried to fire Nanny, she really was a bluff, a kid throwing a tantrum who only wanted to be stopped by someone strong enough to stop her.

Perhaps her seduction of him was motivated by more than pure lust. Perhaps she was truly enamored of him. Would he ever take her as serious competition to his wife?

He would not. He loved Julie more than anyone in the world, loved her more than he had ever loved anyone in his life, shared such experiences and feelings and interests and goals and aversions and passions and prejudices and points of view with Julie that they were not *two* people but *one*—one person who, who . . . ah, the hell with it.

Sure, the passion wasn't there with Julie any longer, but under their present circumstances it could not have been otherwise. The moment her damned episiotomy was thoroughly healed and she wasn't in agony every time he tried to enter her, they'd resume normal sexual relations and the romance would return and they'd be fine again.

Had he met Luci Redman in college as long ago as he'd met Julie, and lived with Luci, and married Luci, and had a baby with Luci, and had Julie been a nanny and come to work for him and Luci, he'd probably be feeling as burnt out and turned off toward *Luci* and as hot for *Julie* as he now . . .

No. He did *not* feel burnt out and turned off toward Julie, he did *not*. He *loved* Julie, and the current cooling of his passion for her was strictly a temporary condition which would pass as soon as they got through this admittedly trying period. And he was *not* hot for Luci Redman, no matter *how* many times she stuck her tongue into his mouth in the shower or fondled his cock under the quilt in the dark or *how* many photographs of him and his wife and child she had in little gold heart-shaped lockets in the bottom of her closet, and that was *that*.

Then he had another idea about the photo in the locket, a somewhat darker one. The idea that Nanny had hidden it away because she was doing something strange with it.

He'd read about people who believed in the occult, who performed strange magical rites over photos of folks they wished to manipulate. Primitive people in Third World countries often refused to be photographed by tourists for this reason—they feared they were vulnerable through their photographic likenesses. It was conceivable that the odd things he'd found in the purse—candles, seeds, sand, incense—were part of some magical ritual which involved the photo in the locket.

And then he wondered whether he wasn't being paranoid. He put everything carefully back in the purse, locked it, left it in the closet in the precise position in which he'd found it and walked quietly out of Nanny's bedroom.

CHAPTER 54

THAT NIGHT Phil cuddled in bed with Julie and imagined it was Nanny, which made him feel miserably, deliciously guilty. Julie was still not in the mood for love, so Phil contented himself with kisses and caresses. After a while he drifted off and found himself in a cabin in the woods with Nanny. Maybe Ralph Roberts's cabin.

It seemed he was married to Nanny, but he was also somehow married to Julie. There had been reports that some sort of huge humanoid beast was loose in the forest. It had been killing and mutilating small animals.

Phil was in bed with Nanny in the cabin in the woods. Nanny was lying on top of Phil, kissing and caressing him, while Julie sat in a straight-backed chair by the side of the bed and looked on approvingly. From somewhere in the rear of the house Harry began to cry. Neither Julie nor Nanny appeared to hear him. Phil extricated himself from Nanny's embrace, got out of bed and rapidly strode back to the baby's room.

Upon entering Harry's room, Phil beheld a grisly sight. The beast from the woods—huge, hairy, wild-eyed, long-fanged—was bending over the baby's crib. Harry's eyes were open, yet he made no sound, even though the monster had gnawed the baby's leg to a bloody stump.

With an animal cry of rage, Phil threw himself upon the beast and began flailing at it with his fists and feet.

Julie was shaking him violently.

"Phil, wake up! Phil!"

Still flailing, he flung himself free of the dream and lay there, gasping.

"Phil, are you awake?"

"Of *course* I'm awake," he said, embarrassed to be caught in a nightmare.

111

"You were screaming and kicking and flailing around," she said. "I was afraid you'd hurt yourself. Or me."

"I'm sorry," he said.

"Do you remember what the dream was about?"

"A monster," he said. "A huge, hairy, wild-eyed monster attacked Harry in his crib. It was gnawing on his leg."

"My God," she said, shuddering.

"I was trying to kill it," he said.

"From the way you were punching and kicking," she said, "I'd guess you were successful."

"Mmmm," he said.

"Your dream is very Oedipal, you know."

"Most are," he said.

They lay in the dark awhile without speaking, and then Julie composed herself for sleep. Phil lay awake for a long time after Julie had resumed her snoring. He remembered the terror of the monster attacking Harry and he remembered the sensuality of Nanny's lovemaking. He was somehow unable to separate the two.

The following morning Julie rose early and left for an appointment with prospective clients on the Upper East Side. Phil had awakened with a bad sore throat and telephoned the office to say he wouldn't be coming in till later in the day, if at all.

As he lay in bed, still thinking about the dream of the previous night and what it meant, he heard a soft tapping at the bedroom door.

"Yes?" he said.

The door opened and Nanny entered.

"Mr. Pressman?"

"Yes, Nanny?"

"I understand you're not feeling very well this morning."

"No, I'm afraid not, Nanny."

"I'm so sorry. Is there anything I can do for you, sir?"

"Not really, but thanks for asking."

She approached the bed.

"Open your mouth and say 'Ah.' "

Phil opened his mouth and said "Ah." Nanny adjusted the bedside lamp and peered down his throat.

"Your throat is a bit inflamed," she said.

"That's not surprising," he said. "I can barely swallow."

"Would you like me to take your temperature?"

"I don't know," he said. "I doubt that I'm running a fever."

Nanny felt his forehead.

"You do feel a little warm."

"Well, go ahead then."

She reached into her pocket, withdrew a thermometer, shook it down with a nurse's practiced snap of the wrist and slipped it between his lips. She picked up his hand and took his pulse for sixty seconds. Then she removed the thermometer, walked over to the window and scrutinized it in the sunlight.

"You have no fever," she said, "but that throat did look quite inflamed. Directly following breakfast I suggest you take two aspirin and gargle with warm water and salt."

"O.K.," said Phil, "I will. And thank you for being concerned about me."

"You don't have to thank me for that, Mr. Pressman," she said. "It's my job. Apart from that, I like you."

"Well, thank you, Nanny. I like you, too."

"Thank you, sir," she said.

She turned to go. As she reached the bedroom door she leaned back in his direction.

"Would you like breakfast in bed, sir?"

"Breakfast in bed?" said Phil delightedly. "Why, yes, Nanny, that would be wonderful."

"Very good, sir."

Nanny smiled shyly. Then she walked back to the bed, lifted Phil's head from his pillow with one hand, and with the other raised her white uniform skirt and then her slip above her waist, lowered her white nylon panties below her knees and guided Phil's face home.

CHAPTER 55

NANNY didn't release Phil's head until he had completely satisfied her with his tongue. When she finally moved away from him he yanked her back again with such force she emitted a raucous laugh. She seized the waistband of his jockey shorts and ripped them to shreds, then straddled his body on the bed and impaled herself upon him.

Just as he was about to climax she came to a dead stop and held him prisoner between her thighs. He felt he could bear the pressure no longer and pleaded with her to move. She moved slightly and he exploded inside of her.

She left him utterly spent. He lay across the bed, drained of sperm and energy, unable to move. He had not had a more exciting sexual encounter in his life. He had never felt more miserable.

It was the first time he had actively pursued her. He berated himself for yanking her back to him when she was trying to leave. He berated himself for doing it with her on the very bed that he and Julie shared.

The phone rang. He picked up the receiver.

"Yeah?" he said.

"Mr. Philip Pressman, please."

"This is Philip Pressman."

"This is the overseas operator, Mr. Pressman. We are ready with your call to London."

"Oh yes, good."

Some metallic sounds, and then a connection.

"Mr. Pressman?"

"Yes, this is Mr. Pressman . . ."

"Ah. Mr. Pressman, this is Miss Higgins at St. Barnabas. I've been checking our staff files here for a Miss Luci Redman, as you requested . . . ?"

"Yes, Miss Higgins . . ."

"We do show a Luci Redman having worked here at St. Barnabas as a nurse, sir . . ."

"You do? Well, good, good. Was it about when I thought? About twelve years ago?"

"Miss Redman was employed at St. Barnabas from 1898 to 1902, sir."

"Excuse me? I didn't quite get that."

"I say Miss Redman was employed here at St. Barnabas from 1898 to 1902."

Phil's first inclination was to laugh, but he didn't wish to insult delicate transatlantic feelings.

"The thing is, Miss Higgins, *our* Miss Redman is about thirty-five, thirty-six years old."

"Is she."

"Yes. If she had worked at St. Barnabas when you say, that would make her over a hundred years old."

"Ah. Quite."

"So I'm afraid it isn't the same woman."

"Quite. Well, that, unfortunately, is the only Luci Redman in our files here, Mr. Pressman. Sorry not to have been more of a help to you."

"Well, thank you anyway for trying."

"Not at all, sir."

Phil hung up the phone and chuckled. Nanny may have had

her faults, he thought, but she's not too bad in the sack for a woman who's over a hundred years old. He wished he could share the joke with Julie.

And then he had a sudden queasy feeling that he could not explain. A feeling that, in some grotesque, wholly incongruous way, the Luci Redman who worked for him and the one who'd worked in St. Barnabas at the turn of the century shared more than a name. The notion was so farfetched and so paranoid he laughed out loud.

CHAPTER 56

BY THE TIME Julie came home from her meeting with the two prospective clients from the Upper East Side, Phil had gargled and consumed enough vitamin C to take the edge off his sore throat, but his guilt over having had sex with Nanny made him so jumpy he didn't know what to do with himself. Making natural-sounding conversation was a task almost beyond his capability.

"Hi, Julie."

"Hi. How's your cold?"

"Better," he said. "How did it go this morning? The meeting, I mean."

"O.K., I guess."

"You think they want to use you or what?"

"I don't know," she said. "They're thinking about it."

"Oh," he said. "When do you think you'll hear?"

"I don't know. In a week or so."

"Oh," he said. "So what are we having for dinner tonight?"

"I don't know. I'll have to ask Nanny what she's planned. Why?"

"Oh, no reason," he said.

"Are you all right?"

"Outside of my throat, you mean? Sure. Why do you ask? I mean why do you ask?"

"You're just so jumpy."

"Jumpy? You're kidding me," he said. "I happen to be having a very relaxing day."

"Oh really? What did you do this morning?"

"This morning?" he said.

"Yes. Don't you remember?"

"Of *course* I remember what I did this morning," he said. "Why wouldn't I remember that?"

"What did you do?"

"I lay around in bed for a while," he said. "Then I had breakfast . . ."

"Yes . . . ?"

"Then I got a phone call from London . . ."

"A phone call from London? Who from?"

"From . . . St. Barnabas Hospital," he said. "They were returning my call, actually. I called them a few days ago. To check up on Nanny. To, you know, check out that she worked there as her résumé said she did."

Julie was frowning at him. He didn't know if this was because he'd been running off at the mouth or because he'd been checking up on Nanny, about whom she had made it quite clear she didn't want to know any more bad things.

"I really wish you hadn't made that call," she said.

"Why not?" he said.

"You know why not."

"Well, I wanted to check her out," he said, "so that's what I did, I made the call."

"And did they say she had worked there?"

"Well, that's the funny part," he said. "I'd told them I thought she worked there about twelve years ago. That's what it said on her résumé, twelve years ago. But when they called me back—"

"Did they say she had worked there or not?" said Julie abruptly.

"I'm just getting to that," he said. "So the woman who called me back said, yes, we do show a Luci Redman having worked at St. Barnabas—"

"Fine," said Julie. "I hope you're satisfied now and can—"

"—but the hilarious thing is that the years she's supposed to have worked there are 1898 to 1902," said Phil. "Isn't that a riot?"

Julie stared at him blankly.

"I mean 1898 to 1902, Julie. That would make her over a hundred years *old*."

Phil chuckled, Julie didn't.

"I just thought it would amuse you," he said. "The idea that they're saying Nanny worked there at the turn of the century."

"What's the point, Phil?"

"What do you mean?" he said.

"I mean what's the point?" she said. "Are you saying that Nanny is a liar? Is that what this is about?"

"No," he said impatiently. "No, that's not the . . . You're missing the whole *point*, for God's sake. I'm just telling you a funny story, Julie. I just thought it would amuse you, that's all."

"O.K.," she said coldly, "I'm amused. I'm positively shaking with mirth. And now, if you don't mind, I'm going to go see about dinner."

Julie went into the kitchen with Nanny.

Phil fumed in silence for several minutes. He didn't understand why Julie was acting so irritably. It couldn't just be because he'd called London after promising not to do any more research on Nanny. Maybe the meeting with the prospective clients from the East Side hadn't gone well.

He heard Harry gooing in the kitchen and he heard Julie and Nanny chatting. Then he heard Julie giggling. He wondered how his wife could be so unfriendly with him one minute and then be giggling with Nanny the next. He wondered what she had to giggle about.

He crept out of the bedroom and into the hallway until he could see into the kitchen. Harry was in his high chair. Julie and Nanny were standing at the kitchen counter, discussing something sotto voce. Their backs were to the doorway. They were holding hands.

CHAPTER 57

A STRANGE QUEASINESS had overtaken Phil. It was a little like seasickness. There was nausea and dizziness and a slight inability to remain standing in perfect balance.

He did not know how to deal with the superbly ironic fact that his wife was now standing in the kitchen, holding hands with the same woman with whom he had been guiltily intimate as recently as this morning. It was entirely possible that their holding hands had no significance and was merely the manifestation of the healthy sisterly camaraderie which existed between women.

It was possible but unlikely. He was reminded of a Hemingway short story called "The Sea Change" which he'd admired in college. A man and woman were breaking up in a bar in Paris. The woman was leaving the man for another woman. The man was not taking it well. The man's name in the story, he realized suddenly, was Phil. "Poor old Phil," he recalled the woman saying at one point.

Nanny put Harry to bed and announced that dinner was ready. Phil went into the living-dining room and took his seat at the table, but the sight of the food made him queasy again.

"What *is* this?" he said, pointing to his plate.

"Eggplant," said Nanny.

"Eggplant?" said Phil.

"It's very nutritious," said Nanny defensively.

"Nanny, I thought I told you I'm *allergic* to eggplant," said Phil. "Didn't I tell you the last time we had eggplant that I'm allergic to it?"

"You didn't say you were allergic to it," said Julie. "You said you didn't *like* it. If you'd said you were *allergic* to it, Nanny wouldn't have made it for you again, would you, Nanny?"

"Why do you have to take her side?" said Phil. "Can't Nanny speak for herself?"

"I'm not taking anybody's side," said Julie, "and I wish you'd stop acting like a child."

"I'm not acting like a child," said Phil. "I'm acting like an adult who's allergic to eggplant."

"No you're not," said Julie. "You're acting like a child."

Phil knew he was acting like a child, but he couldn't seem to be able to stop himself. He pushed his chair away from the table and strode into the bedroom and slammed the door. Then he opened the bedroom door, strode to the hall closet and grabbed his coat.

"Where are you going?" said Julie.

"Out," said Phil, walking to the front door.

"Out where?" said Julie.

"Out to eat something besides eggplant," said Phil, jerking open the front door.

"This isn't about eggplant," said Julie, but Phil had already slammed the door behind him.

CHAPTER 58

PHIL went for a walk in the neighborhood to think. It was extremely cold. A fine powdery snow had begun to fall. It was not the best neighborhood in the city in which to think. It was not the best neighborhood in the city in which to walk, particularly after dark. Normal people deserted this area every day several hours before nightfall. Anybody who was on the street now was probably looking for painful and violent sex with someone of the same gender. A fitting place for Phil to think about what he had to think about.

Phil was reasonably certain that something was going on between Julie and Nanny, but he wasn't sure what. It might not have gotten sexual yet. If allowed to continue, it eventually could. He didn't think that Julie was attracted to women. He was sure that whatever was going on between them was entirely Nanny's doing.

His guess was that Nanny was seducing Julie the same way that she seduced him, and that the point of both seductions was control. He was surprised Nanny had been able to seduce him so easily. He had really thought his convictions about monogamy were stronger than they'd proven to be. He was surprised Nanny had gotten as far as she had with Julie. Under normal circumstances, he thought, Julie wouldn't even have been approachable.

Their present circumstances weren't normal, of course. The discomfort of marital sex and the close proximity of as powerful and seductive a personality as Nanny had made both Phil and Julie a lot more vulnerable than they would ordinarily have been. But even that didn't explain the ease with which Nanny had been able to take such control of their lives.

Perhaps Nanny had been able to accomplish all she'd accomplished because she'd been employing some sort of power that they weren't even aware of. Some form of subconscious or subliminal

or post-hypnotic suggestion. Some psychic or mystical or para-
normal influence. Phil wasn't sure he believed such things existed,
but if they did, and if Nanny was using something of that nature
on them, it would, at the very least, get him off the hook with his
conscience.

He wished he could talk to somebody about this. A friend or
—Julie would love this—a shrink. He'd talked about Nanny once
to Ralph Roberts, and that had been mildly satisfying. He wouldn't
think of trusting Roberts with the suspicion that something might
be going on between Julie and Nanny, or the one that Nanny might
be using some psychic powers on Julie or himself. He'd never
trusted any man to really level with him. His most vulnerable
secrets he'd always entrusted to women. First his mother, then
various strong maternal figures. Besides Nanny, there were currently no strong maternal figures in Phil's life. Except for Mary
Margaret Sullivan, of course.

He liked Mary Margaret. He knew it was a dubious idea to go
to an employer with one's personal problems, but he felt she'd be
understanding and wise about them if he did. He knew she'd be
able to cut through his paranoia, if paranoia it was, as she had with
his temporary hysteria about decaffeination processes. He was ex-
periencing a form of mild hysteria now about Nanny and Julie.
Maybe all he needed was somebody to calm him down. Mary
Margaret *had* said if he ever wanted to discuss anything with her
in the future, she'd listen, hadn't she?

He wondered if it would hurt just to have a general sort of
conversation with her—nothing too specific, just a sort of casual,
free-form chat. Even that would be reassuring. He had felt very
calm and reassured after the chat about decaffeination. He had a
sudden longing to talk to Mary Margaret that he couldn't rationally
explain, but he didn't have her home number and he doubted she
was listed in the Manhattan directory. You never knew, though,
who was listed in the Manhattan directory and who was not.

At the end of the block, under a sodium vapor streetlight, was
an open-style phone booth. He walked down to the booth and

dialed Information. As he waited for an operator to come on the line, a figure in black leather emerged from the shadows about ten yards away.

Oh, great, he thought, just what I need.

Information had still not picked up. Phil weighed the advisability of hanging up and beating it out of there to avoid a confrontation with the leather person, then decided he was not going to be intimidated.

The figure slid closer. It was a tall, well-built man wearing black leather pants, a black motorcycle jacket with many zippers and chains, a black leather cap with a bill, high black leather boots, black leather gloves and aviator sunglasses. The man was staring quite obviously in Phil's direction and moving closer.

"Information, may I help you?" said the operator.

"Yes," said Phil, keeping a wary eye on the biker or whatever he was. "A listing for Sullivan, Mary Margaret Sullivan, on Central Park West?"

"One moment, please," said the operator.

The biker slid closer and said something in a husky voice.

"What?" said Phil, instantly realizing the stupidity of acknowledging the creature's presence.

"I said why call Mary Margaret when you could have *me?*"

Phil was extremely uncomfortable at the man's moronic pickup attempt. Phil hadn't asked to be hit on, he was just making a phone call.

"Don't you think I'm more attractive than Mary Margaret?" said the biker.

Oh God, thought Phil, is this what women have to put up with from men all their lives?

"I show a listing for an M. M. Sullivan on Central Park West," said the operator. "Would that be it?"

"That sounds right," said Phil delightedly.

"Excellent," said the biker, misunderstanding Phil's utterance and moving within a foot of the phone booth.

The female robot employed by the phone company announced

the number. Phil hung up just as the biker slipped an arm through his. Phil heard his pulse start pounding in his ears.

"If you don't take your arm away *immediately*," said Phil in a loud, terse voice which he did not recall owning, "I will drive your nose up into your brain."

"Oh, *honey*, *take* me, I'm *yours!*" said the biker, but he withdrew his arm and moved a step backward and Phil realized with satisfaction that he'd frightened him.

Phil turned on his heel and walked in the opposite direction. The biker followed him three yards behind.

"Tell me again what you're going to do to me, honey," said the biker.

Phil whirled about.

"If you don't start running before I count three," said Phil in the same amazing voice, shoving his hand flamboyantly into his empty jacket pocket, "I am going to put six .357 magnum bullets right between your fucking eyes and splatter your brains all over the street! *One!* . . . *Two!* . . ."

The biker took off down the block so fast Phil was astonished he could move so rapidly in all that leather. With his heart thundering in his chest, Phil watched the biker's retreat with an animal sense of victory.

If only I could be that strong at home, he thought.

CHAPTER 59

JULIE stared at the slammed door, then sagged inward in her seat. She sat looking at her plate for several seconds longer, then got up and walked into the bedroom and flung herself onto the bed.

After a few minutes, Nanny walked to the bedroom door and, although it was not closed, tapped on it.

"Yes, Nanny?" said Julie into the bedspread.

Nanny walked into the room and stood beside the bed. Julie was crying quietly, her tears forming a spreading wet spot under her face.

"Mr. Pressman isn't feeling well," said Nanny. "That's why he is acting like a child."

Julie shook her head.

"Mr. Pressman is acting like a child because Mr. Pressman *is* a child," she said, continuing to cry.

"Ssshhhh," said Nanny, bending down and patting Julie's back.

"*All* men are such goddam *children*," said Julie. "I swear to God, I've never met a single man who was a grownup in my entire *life*."

"Would you prefer to be alone now, Mrs. Pressman?" said Nanny.

"No," said Julie. "Please stay a minute longer, Nanny."

Nanny sat down on the bed beside Julie. After a moment she lifted Julie's head onto her lap. Nanny began stroking Julie's hair.

"That feels good," said Julie.

Nanny continued stroking Julie's hair. Julie stopped sniffling and tried to relax.

"Would you like me to draw you a bubble bath?" said Nanny.

"No thank you," said Julie.

"How about a nice massage?"

Julie thought about this a moment.

"You know," said Julie, "I think that would really be the perfect thing now. Thank you, Nanny."

Nanny went into the Pressmans' bathroom and returned with two large bath sheets and a bottle of Swiss Formula moisturizing lotion. Julie had already drawn back the covers and was taking off her clothes. Nanny helped her finish undressing, then had her lie face down on one of the towels and began working the lotion into Julie's skin.

Julie sighed and groaned as Nanny slowly and methodically proceeded across her tightly corded body, releasing the tension in the muscles, working out the kinks, spreading the warmth and the looseness and the relaxation toward the tips of her fingers, the tips of her toes, stroking her masterfully into a marvelous, dreamy, twilight trance.

When Nanny was through with Julie's back she tenderly turned her over and began working on her front. Her eyes glued shut, Julie was dimly aware of Nanny's hands on her arms, her shoulders, her stomach, her thighs, on every part of her body, spreading the warm glow outward to her extremities, causing her skin to tingle, causing her nipples to stiffen as Nanny's warm fingers continued to rub the slippery lotion into her flesh.

Below the layers of velvet darkness where Nanny had pushed her, Julie was vaguely, dreamily puzzled. She didn't recall any masseuse ever rubbing lotion into her breasts like that before, didn't recall the growing tingle like the one which was beginning to make itself felt between her thighs. She didn't think that Nanny had touched her pubic mound, or if she had, that it had been anything more than the lightest, fastest flutter of fingers over the area. Julie was so drowsy and her entire being was in such a state of bliss that she couldn't bear ascending to any level of consciousness high enough to consider the question seriously.

CHAPTER 60

"GOOD EVENING, Pressman," said Mary Margaret Sullivan, "I'm glad you came."

Phil entered self-consciously and shook hands with his boss.

"I'm sorry for barging in on you like this," said Phil, "especially at dinner hour, but I really—"

"Not at all, not at all," said Mary Margaret, shutting the door and locking three locks of a variety Phil hadn't seen before. "And I'm through with dinner. In fact, this is about the time I generally start work."

"Oh," said Phil, "I'm sorry. Maybe we ought to arrange a more convenient time to talk."

"Nonsense," she said, "I'm desperate for any excuse not to work."

"O.K.," said Phil.

She led him into the large high-ceilinged living room. Shelves of books rose to the ceiling on two walls. On another wall hung a lethal-looking sword from Japan. There were also several small, rather familiar-looking paintings. He took a closer look at the paintings and realized, with a tiny surge of excitement, that they were mostly original Manets, Monets and Picassos.

"Very nice," he said, inclining his head toward the artwork.

"One of the perks of owning a successful business," she said. "Would you like a drink?"

"No thanks," said Phil, and then regretted his response. "I haven't had anything to eat, but maybe a little brandy would warm me up."

"I can fix you some brandy, and I can also fix you something to eat," she said.

"I wouldn't want you to go to any trouble," he said.

"Neither would I," she said. "Come into the kitchen and let me fix you some leftover chicken."

Smiling at how easily he'd managed to get her to play the mother role for him, he followed her into the kitchen and watched her prepare his food.

"So," she said, heating up the chicken, "you didn't come here looking for dinner. Why *did* you come here tonight?"

"Well," said Phil uneasily, "I just needed a friend to talk to, I guess."

"I assume, since you're not discussing whatever it is with your wife," she said, "that she is part of what you wanted to talk about."

Phil smiled.

"Yeah."

"Well," she said, "why don't you tell me all about it? And then afterwards I shall render an opinion."

"Fair enough," said Phil.

For the next hour, as he ate his chicken and sipped his brandy, Phil told her, as candidly as he was able, everything that had happened to him and Julie, from the moment Nanny moved into their apartment in the wholesale meat district.

At first he was reluctant to tell her about the sex, but she was so receptive and supportive about everything else that he decided it was probably important she know all that had happened if she were to help. If Mary Margaret was shocked by his revelations she hid it as well as any psychiatrist.

At last Phil finished his story and stopped to hear her reaction. She did not immediately respond.

"So," said Phil uneasily, "what's the verdict? Is my wife having an affair with our nanny or am I just being paranoid?"

"When you first began your story," she said, "I thought it was just going to be the standard confession of a guilt-ridden husband baring his soul about seducing a hot-pantsed household employee . . ."

"Yes . . ." said Phil, reddening.

"But it's a bit worse than that, isn't it?" she said. "At the very least, your nanny is manipulating you sexually. I doubt that she's seducing your wife, but she has certainly seduced *you*, in a pretty outrageous and foolhardy manner. I think that's pretty tacky behavior for a nanny. I doubt she was breast-feeding your baby, because it's physically impossible, but I do think it's strange she was taking a bath with him. If it were me, I'd get rid of her."

"But my wife has grown very attached to her," said Phil. "My wife has convinced herself we can't get along without her."

"So you say. But your wife may not be the best judge of what's good for her or you or for the baby. I think you ought to have a serious talk with your wife. I think you ought to tell her about our discussion and suggest that keeping Nanny in your household may pose a threat to all of you. Tell her everything you told me."

"Everything?" said Phil dubiously.

"Everything."

"You're not suggesting I tell her about the sex?" said Phil.

Mary Margaret nodded.

"Everything," she said. "Make a clean breast of it. She'll be quite hurt at first, but I think it will help her realize the seriousness of what you're telling her and she may begin to see the sort of person your nanny really is."

Phil sighed.

"Julie is an extremely jealous person," said Phil. "I don't think she's going to be able to hear anything else if I tell her about the sex."

"Well, that's something you'll have to determine for yourself then," said Mary Margaret. "But you must tell her about our discussion and urge her to let the nanny go."

"You really think that's necessary?" said Phil.

"I wouldn't suggest it if I didn't."

"O.K.," said Phil, taking a last sip of brandy and getting up from the counter. "Well, thank you for taking the time to talk to me. I guess I'd better let you get back to your work."

"Is that all you wanted to ask me?" she said.

"Actually . . . actually not," he said.

"What else did you want to ask me?"

"Well," he said, "this is going to sound a little off the wall, but . . ."

"Yes . . . ?"

"Well, I had a notion that Nanny might be more than a seducer. I had a notion that she's something, uh, more sinister than that."

"What do you mean?"

"Well," said Phil, "I started thinking that the letters of recommendation she'd given us might be phony, that she'd written them herself on stolen stationery. I went through her things, looking for something to corroborate that—like maybe a few sheets of *our* stationery—and I found some eerie stuff."

"What did you find?"

"I don't know. Candles. Sand. Incense. Little seeds. An antique gold locket with our photo inside it."

"Candles, sand, incense, seeds and a photo of you in a locket?" she said. "That doesn't sound eerie to *me*."

"Well, there were other things, too, now that I think about it."

"Go on."

"I called a hospital in London that she claimed to have worked at about twelve years ago. They didn't have any record of a Luci Redman working there then, but they did have someone with her name who worked there around the turn of the century . . ."

Mary Margaret looked at him quizzically.

"I don't know if I'm following this," she said.

"At first I thought it was funny that somebody with the same name had worked there at the turn of the century and all," said Phil. "But then I started to get this very spooky feeling . . ."

"Surely you're not saying you think it's the same woman?"

"I know it's crazy," said Phil, "but something about her lately has started giving me the creeps."

"And it makes you think she's—what?—some kind of supernatural creature?"

"The thought has crossed my mind," said Phil.

Mary Margaret Sullivan shook her head and laughed.

"So you think I'm being paranoid," said Phil.

"What I think, Pressman, is that you have a very active imagination," she said. "Which is very valuable in a copywriter—so long as it doesn't make him imagine that the coffee he's selling causes cancer, or that the nurse who takes care of his baby is a member of the walking undead."

"O.K.," said Phil. "Got it. Well, now I really *am* going to leave and let you get back to work."

"If I must," she said.

She walked with him to the door and unlocked the three locks.

"Thanks for the chicken and the brandy," he said.

"Don't mention it."

"And thanks again for listening to me," he said. "There wasn't anybody else I felt I could go to."

"I hope it helped," she said.

"Oh, it did. It really did."

"Anytime," she said. "And do let me know what happens."

"Oh, I will," said Phil.

She regarded him thoughtfully and smiled.

"I like you, Pressman. You're a little more neurotic than I'm comfortable with, but you're a really nice young man."

"Thank you," he said. "I like you, too."

"If you ever want to talk some more, please don't hesitate to ask me," she said. "I'm in the office three days a week, and at home I work quite late. I'd be only too glad to help bring you back to reality when you find yourself slipping away."

"Thanks," said Phil with a self-conscious smile, "I could probably use that."

"If I'm not in, just leave a message on my answering machine and I'll get back to you as soon as I receive it."

Phil shook hands with her, then impulsively kissed her on the cheek. She blushed and smiled and kissed *him* on the cheek. Then he walked through the front door and took the self-service elevator down to the street.

He felt reassured by his talk with Mary Margaret Sullivan. He no longer feared that Nanny was seducing Julie, and he had to admit that the idea of Nanny as anything more than human was pretty absurd. He agreed that they should get rid of Nanny as soon as possible. He would talk it over with Julie and get her to understand.

He walked along Central Park West, looking for a taxi. The night had turned colder and he put his collar up against the stiff wind whipping across the park. The fine powdery snow which was falling earlier had turned thicker and heavier. Phil recalled someone saying that six to eight inches were expected before morning.

That meant the city would come to a standstill, he thought. People in Chicago took six to eight inches of snow in stride and went about their regular business. People in New York, he had discovered, reacted to snow as though they'd never seen it before.

A cab approached with its dome light on, but when Phil tried to signal it to stop it ignored him. Cabdrivers, he thought, like all other trades in New York, don't really need the work. He shrugged and continued walking.

CHAPTER 61

BY THE TIME Phil got home the apartment was dark and everybody appeared to be asleep.

He went into Harry's room to make sure he was all right. He shone a penlight on the baby, who was sleeping on his stomach, with his knees tucked under him and his behind sticking up into the air.

He adjusted Harry's blanket so that it was covering his body and moved it away from his face to make sure he didn't suffocate. He watched Harry sleep and wondered if there would ever be a time when he no longer had colic, when he reacted as eagerly to Phil's presence as he did to Nanny's and Julie's.

It was difficult to be the outsider. Phil wanted so much to be accepted by his son, to be able to cuddle him without making him cry, to feel Harry loved him or liked him or responded to him in some pleasurable way, to feel that he was actually the boy's father.

As he looked at the baby in the crib Phil realized he had automatically started to sway. He had spent so many nights holding Harry and swaying back and forth to comfort him that he now swayed even when he wasn't holding him.

Soon it would be time for Harry's inoculations against diphtheria, pertussis and tetanus. Phil had heard news stories about the terrible reactions some babies had to DPT shots—convulsions, collapse, brain damage, the worst. If Harry got the shots he could be brain damaged for life. If he didn't get the shots he could get diphtheria or tetanus and die. Only a small percentage of the babies who got DPT shots suffered brain damage, but what if Harry was one of them? He had to stop thinking such thoughts. He had to stop imagining the worst.

Phil leaned over the crib and gave the baby a kiss. Harry made a sleepy noise and Phil withdrew, afraid he might wake and begin his ceaseless crying.

Phil walked back to his own bedroom in the dark, let himself quietly in the door, felt his way along the bedroom wall into the bathroom, felt his way along the bathroom wall to the sink. He located his toothbrush and a tube of toothpaste in the dark, brushed his teeth and washed his face, then felt his way out of the bathroom and along the bedroom wall to the bed. He stripped off his clothes, deposited them on the carpet and climbed under the covers as quietly as he could.

"I'm awake," said Julie in a normal voice.

"Oh," said Phil. "Did I wake you?"

"No," she said. "I couldn't sleep. I've been wondering where you were."

"Really?"

"Yes."

"Well, I would have called to tell you, but frankly I didn't care all that much if you worried. I was pretty angry with you."

"I know you were," she said.

"Good."

"Phil?"

"Yeah?"

"I . . . feel really bad about the way we've been with each other lately."

A sigh.

"Me too," he said.

"I hate the way we've been talking to each other. It sounds so unloving. It's . . . not the way I feel."

"Really?" he said. "I was beginning to wonder."

"Really."

She moved against him and put her arms around his neck. He hugged her.

"Where did you go tonight?" she said.

He hesitated.

"I'll tell you, but I don't want you to get upset."

"Why would I be upset?"

"I just think you might be," he said.

"Go ahead and tell me and we'll see."

"O.K.," he said. "I went to see Mary Margaret Sullivan."

A pause.

"The president of your agency?"

"Right."

A long pause.

"So," she said, "does that mean I have competition?"

At first he didn't understand her question, and then he did and burst into laughter.

"May I be let in on the joke?" she said with exaggerated coolness.

"I'm sorry," he said. "It never occurred to me you might be jealous of a woman who's sixty-five years old."

"Mary Margaret Sullivan is sixty-five years old?"

"Yes."

She giggled.

"Thank God," she said.

"I sure wish you had more confidence," he said. "In me and in yourself."

"So do I," she said. "God. Well, what did you go to see her for? Was it about one of the ads you're writing?"

"You're not going to like it," he said.

"Tell me anyway."

"O.K.," he said. "I went to talk to her about what's been going on between you and me and Nanny."

She sighed.

"You were right," she said. "I don't like it."

"In any case," he said, "that's what I did."

"What did she tell you?"

"She said Nanny sounded manipulative and inappropriate. She thought we ought to get rid of her."

Another pause.

"And what do *you* think?"

"I think she's right."

Neither of them said anything for a while.

"Phil?"

"Yeah, babe?"

"I love you."

"I love you too," he said.

They hugged. He idly caressed her back awhile. After a few minutes he tried moving the caresses down toward her buttocks in hopes of effecting a smooth transition into foreplay. But when he got below her waist she yawned and, holding his arms firmly in place around her, turned over and settled in for sleep.

He lay awake holding her. His arm underneath her grew cold, numb and prickly, and then he fell asleep. Shortly afterwards he was aware she'd turned back to him and begun to caress his face and arms. In his groggy state he knew she'd been lying there awake, feeling guilty about rejecting him, and was now dutifully trying to respond to him. He didn't want lovemaking motivated by guilt. He elected to remain asleep.

He awoke an hour or so later to the realization that their bedroom door was ajar. Enough light was coming into the room from somewhere in the apartment for him to clearly make out Nanny in her white uniform, standing motionless just inside the doorway, facing the bed.

Here we go again, he thought bitterly.

Gazing in Phil's direction, Nanny took a step toward the bed, unzipped her uniform and let it drop to the carpet. Then she stepped out of her shoes, pushed down her slip, unhooked her bra and stepped out of her panties.

She was completely naked. She took another step toward the bed. Phil held up his hand as a signal for her not to come closer.

Nanny emitted a contemptuous laugh. Then she stuck her fingers into her eyes and began peeling her face down from her forehead like a rubber mask, revealing popping eyeballs and a shiny wet skull covered with pulp.

CHAPTER 62

THE SCREAM was the most piercing he had ever heard, and when Julie began shaking him he realized it was coming from his own throat, but he couldn't at first make it stop, and Julie was yelling for him to wake up.

Eventually he did wake up, and was terrified to look at the place where Nanny had stood a moment before, staring at him with eyeballs popping out of their sockets, rows of gleaming skeletal teeth unframed by the already peeled-off lips.

But Nanny was gone and the bedroom door was once more closed. It was certain that Nanny had never been there to begin with, that it had truly been a nightmare, but Phil couldn't stop his teeth from chattering.

Julie held him in her arms, making shooshing noises, patting his back and trying to comfort him, until finally he relaxed.

In the back bedroom the baby had awakened as a result of Phil's screaming and begun to cry.

"Another nightmare?" said Julie gently.

"I hope so," he said.

"What was it this time?"

He considered the dream a moment before replying.

"I don't think you'd want me to describe it," he said.

"Why not?"

"I don't think you'd care much for the imagery," he said.

CHAPTER 63

DURING THE NIGHT eight inches of snow fell on New York. By morning the sanitation department was in a panic. A snow emergency had been declared. A pathetically small squadron of snowplows and salt spreaders had been deployed to do battle with the strange cold white stuff. Garbage collection had been suspended indefinitely as the garbagemen left for the front lines.

Phil awoke at dawn after an exhausting and disquieting dream he couldn't quite remember. He began to mull over his discussion of the previous evening with Mary Margaret Sullivan and his own paranoid fears of the occult.

Regardless of whether or not Nanny had been up to anything occult, they had to get rid of her. And the conversation about it with Julie the previous night had not, he felt, been conclusive.

As he sat on the bed, gazing down at Julie, she stirred, looked up, saw him and smiled.

"Hi," she said brightly, giving him a kiss.

"Hi."

"What time is it?"

"About seven-twenty," he said. "Julie, we've got to talk."

"Sure. Why so grim?"

"You know what we discussed last night? About Nanny?"

"Yes . . . ?"

"Well, I've been awake since dawn and I've been giving it a hell of a lot of thought. Julie, I think that Nanny is, at best, a deeply disturbed person. I think we have to get rid of her right away—before she does something to Harry."

Julie looked suddenly drained.

"I'm sorry," he said. "I know how that must make you feel."

She nodded.

"Phil," she said, "how are we going to get along without her?"

138

"We'll manage. We'll get somebody else to help with Harry, or we can do it ourselves. Remember how we always planned to do it ourselves?"

She took his hand.

"You're really serious about this, aren't you?" she said.

"Julie, I think Nanny is a threat—to our baby and also . . . to our marriage."

Julie frowned.

"To our marriage?" she said. "In what way is she a threat to our marriage?"

Phil said nothing.

"In what way is she a threat to our marriage, Phil?"

"Nanny is, as far as I can see . . . actively seducing both of us," he said.

Julie was silent a moment.

"I see," she said. "And has she succeeded?"

A pause.

"Has she succeeded, Phil?"

"You tell *me*," he said.

"She hasn't with me," she said.

"Good."

"What about with you?" she said.

He didn't reply. She continued to look at him.

"Phil?"

He remained silent. Her eyes began to fill with tears.

"All right then, get rid of her," she said, in a flat, dead voice, and buried her face in her pillow.

CHAPTER 64

WHEN HE FIRED HER *this* time, Phil thought, it was going to have to stick. It was going to have to be done swiftly and surely and with no ambivalence. His sexual ambivalence last time had given her an opening through which to escape. There would be no ambivalence this time, sexual or otherwise. If he couldn't get rid of her now he risked danger to Julie and the baby, and he would never tolerate that.

When Nanny came back from her morning walk with Harry, Phil went into the baby's room. Nanny was removing Harry's snowsuit.

"Nanny, I have something important to say."

"Yes, Mr. Pressman?"

"Mrs. Pressman and I have come to a very difficult decision. . . ."

"Yes, Mr. Pressman?"

"We've decided we have to let you go after all."

Nanny continued undressing the baby and gave no indication that she had heard.

"Did you hear what I said, Nanny? We're letting you go," he said. "We feel it would be best if you left as soon as possible."

"My my my," she said. "This is so *sudden*, Mr. Pressman."

"Yes."

"What, may I ask, inspired such a sudden and ill-conceived notion?"

"It doesn't matter what inspired it," he said. "The only important thing is that you understand that you must leave right away. Preferably by the end of the day."

"Is this what they refer to in corporate life as a 'sudden death termination'?" she said, smiling.

"Under the circumstances, it's the best way for all concerned."

"It's not best for *me*," she said.

"Then I'm sorry," he said. "But it's still the way that we're going to do it."

She continued changing the baby's clothes.

"May I inquire why I am being dismissed?" she said.

"It's a number of things," he said.

"List them."

"I'd rather not."

"Surely you can tell me why you are dismissing me," she said. "Surely you owe me that much. After the intimacy we've shared."

"Oh, that's great," he said with a sarcastic laugh, " 'after the intimacy we've shared.' "

"You find our intimacy amusing, do you?" she said.

"I find our intimacy isn't very intimate," he said. "I think you'd share intimacy with a . . . a hall tree."

She slapped his face so hard he almost lost his balance. Harry screamed.

"How *dare* you speak to me in such a manner!" she said in a hiss. "How *dare* you!"

"I suppose you haven't been seducing my wife as surely as you've been seducing me!" he said.

She snorted.

"So that's it, is it?" she said. "You honestly believe I've been seducing your wife?"

"Haven't you?" he said.

"Hardly," she said.

"Right."

"For your information, Mr. Pressman," she said, "your wife is scarcely able to keep her chubby little hands off my body."

"What?"

"Your wife has an embarrassing crush on me," she said. "She moons over me like a lovesick schoolboy. If any seduction is going on there, I can assure you it has not originated with *me*."

Phil stared at her, unable to speak.

"What do you think I am," said Nanny, "a bloody lesbian?"

"I have no idea what you are," he said, "and I don't think I *want* to know. But I do want you out of this household by the end of the day."

She collected herself.

"Then you are quite serious about this?" she said.

"Completely serious," he said.

A pause.

"I shall leave this household at a time and in a manner of my own choosing," she said.

CHAPTER 65

PHIL called into the office to say he was feeling ill and would be working at home for a while. When he went back into the bedroom to tell Julie of the firing he saw that she had gone back to sleep.

It was unlike her to sleep so late. At about noon Julie staggered into the kitchen for a light breakfast. Phil asked if she was feeling O.K., and she answered him monosyllabically.

After breakfast she went back to bed, where she remained till after 4 p.m. At 4:20 she got up again for lunch and seemed weaker than before. Once again he tried to talk to her, and once again she was not responsive.

He supposed she was reacting to his tacit admission he'd let Nanny seduce him, and so he didn't press her. He felt guilty enough, and he knew how jealous she was. Nanny's allegation about Julie trying to seduce her was utter nonsense. Julie wasn't a seducer—not of men, and certainly not of women.

At the end of the day Julie seemed no better, and Nanny had

made no visible moves to leave. If Nanny did indeed leave, and if Julie continued in her somnambulism, Phil would, by default, become the sole caretaker of a colicky baby, a prospect which he viewed with little enthusiasm.

By dinner time Julie appeared too weak to rise at all. Phil took her temperature and found her subnormal. He asked her again if she was O.K. and received no satisfactory response. He brought her some food on a tray and she could barely manage to get it down. Phil was becoming alarmed.

The following day Julie was no better, and Nanny had still made no apparent plans to depart. She continued to take care of Harry and do household chores just as though she were still working for them.

Phil told his office he was still under the weather and would continue working at home, then he telephoned a doctor and described Julie's symptoms, but all the physician could advise was to bring her in for an examination.

Julie wasn't interested in going to see the doctor, and Phil wasn't anxious to force her. Also he was not eager to leave Nanny alone with Harry, afraid he might return home to find them both gone. If his parents or Julie's had lived in New York, he could have asked *them* to take Julie to the doctor. If his parents or Julie's had lived in New York, they might not have had to hire a nanny in the first place.

Phil tried to think of a friend who could take Julie to the doctor and realized all their friends were in Chicago. They'd been so focused on the pregnancy and the birth and the colic that they'd had little time for the outside world. They'd befriended nobody in New York, not even a neighbor, not even a couple in their Lamaze class. Mary Margaret Sullivan was about the closest thing to a friend that Phil had, and he didn't really think he could ask her to take his wife to the doctor.

Phil decided to sit tight and see if Julie's condition improved without going to the doctor.

Toward evening the telephone rang. Phil picked it up.

"I have a person-to-person call for Mr. Pressman," said an operator's voice.

"Yes," said Phil, "all right."

"Is this Mr. Pressman?" said the operator.

"It is," said Phil.

"Go ahead, sir," said the operator to the caller.

There was no immediate response from the other end of the line.

"Hello?" said Phil. "Are you there?"

"Mr. Pressman?" said a man's voice. It sounded oddly hollow and distracted.

"Yes," said Phil, "who is this?"

"This is William Parsons."

"Mr. Parsons!" said Phil excitedly. "Thank you for getting back to me! Listen, I'm sorry to have bothered you at a time which I understand must be quite difficult for you, but I had a number of questions which I—"

"Mr. Pressman," said Parsons much more forcefully, cutting him short, "I'm afraid I must be brief. Is the Redman woman still working for you?"

"No," said Phil. "Well, yes and no."

"Is it yes or is it no?"

"Technically, no," said Phil. "I fired her."

"Has she left the premises yet?"

"Well, no. She said she— "

"Do you know when she is planning to leave?"

"Not really," said Phil. "She said she was going to leave in a time and manner of her own choosing."

There was a short silence at the other end of the line.

"You must get her out *now*," said Parsons.

"Well, I'd like to," said Phil, "but I'm not exactly sure how to go about it. I mean, if I go to the police and tell them I fired my nanny but she refuses to leave my apartment, I'm going to be laughed out of the precinct house. I suppose I could throw her out bodily, but—"

"*No!*" said Parsons. "Don't, under *any* circumstances, force a physical confrontation."

"Why not?" said Phil.

"Can you take your wife and baby and leave the apartment without her seeing you?"

"What, you mean leave her the apartment?" said Phil incredulously.

"No, just go away somewhere for a while," said Parsons. "She's not going to stay there very long without you. It's not the apartment she wants. Can you leave now?"

"Well, I suppose so," said Phil, "but my wife is extremely weak right now and—"

"Excuse me," said Parsons, "your wife is extremely *what?*"

"Weak. Why?"

"When did she become weak?"

"Yesterday," said Phil.

"Was it before or after you told Miss Redman she would have to leave?"

"After. Why?"

"Because the reason she feels weak is Miss Redman's doing. Listen to me," said Parsons grimly. "You have got to get your wife and baby out of there *immediately.*"

"Well, I know you're probably right about that," said Phil, "but—"

"No, I mean *immediately,*" said Parsons.

"Why?"

"Your lives are in danger," said Parsons.

"What are you saying?"

"*I am saying if you don't leave there immediately she will kill you,*" said Parsons and hung up.

CHAPTER 66

PULSE pounding in his ears, Phil entered his bedroom and leaned over Julie in bed and tried to shake her awake. She groaned but did not open her eyes.

"Julie," Phil whispered harshly into her ear, "we have to leave here right away, you and I and Harry. Do you think you could walk with my help?"

Julie said something too faint to be intelligible.

"What?" said Phil.

"Why?" said Julie weakly.

"I can't explain now," said Phil. "But we have to leave immediately. Do you think you can walk if I help you?"

"Where . . . are we going?" said Julie.

"It doesn't matter," said Phil. "Just tell me if you think you can walk with my help."

"I . . . could try," said Julie weakly.

"Good girl," said Phil.

Phil helped Julie to sit up and dress in warm clothing. Then he pulled on a warm sweater, his down jacket and boots, and quietly walked down the hall to Nanny's and Harry's bedrooms.

No light was visible from beneath Nanny's door. This was promising. There was a good chance that Nanny had already gone to sleep. If only Harry were as sleepy as he usually was when Phil gave him his night bottle, perhaps he wouldn't cry and wake Nanny.

Phil put his hand on the doorknob and slowly turned it, then carefully pushed the door inward. It creaked slightly on its hinges. Phil stepped cautiously into the room, hearing a floorboard squeak slightly under the carpeting.

There was no sound from Harry's cradle. So far so good. But it was so dark he risked crashing into something and waking both

Harry and Nanny. Phil decided to risk the night-light. He felt his way to the wall, and along the wall to the changing table, and then just above the changing table to the night-light.

He snapped on the night-light and was just about to reach into the cradle for the baby when he saw her. Sitting in the rocking chair next to the cradle. Watching them carefully. Nanny.

CHAPTER 67

"WHAT DO YOU THINK you're doing?" said Nanny in a chilling voice.

The shock of discovering her in this manner had set Phil's heart thudding in his chest.

"I just wanted to see how Harry was doing," Phil said.

"You wanted to see how Harry was doing?" said Nanny.

"Yes," said Phil.

Harry woke up and began crying in a tentative manner.

"You see what you've done now?" said Nanny. "You've awakened him."

Harry's crying became less tentative.

"He's my *son*, for Christ's sake," said Phil. "I can wake him or do whatever the hell else I like with him!"

Harry began to scream. Nanny arose from the rocking chair and picked him up. The screaming and crying ceased immediately.

"Is there anything more you would like to see?" said Nanny.

Phil met Nanny's hostile glare. He was about to say something incendiary, then he remembered Parsons's firm warning not to force a physical confrontation and decided that might be wise, especially with Harry in the room.

"Not just now," said Phil, and turned and left the room.

CHAPTER 68

WELL, she's won this round, Phil thought as he headed back to his bedroom. She'd apparently been expecting something like this. There wasn't much more he could do tonight, but perhaps he could get her out of the house on some pretext tomorrow and sneak out then.

He got Julie undressed and back under the covers. She was so weak she didn't press him for an explanation of what was going on.

Before Phil went to bed he checked all the locks on the front door. Then he moved a heavy desk up against the door, reasoning that if Nanny tried to sneak out with the baby, the noise and difficulty of moving the desk would alert him. He wasn't sure what means he would use to stop her, though.

He ran the disturbing conversation with Parsons over and over again in his mind. Clearly, Parsons was terrified of Nanny. Phil wasn't sure why. She didn't *seem* dangerous. If she'd wanted to hurt them, she'd had ample opportunity before this. It was possible that Parsons was a lunatic. And yet the tone of his voice on the phone had made Phil's flesh crawl. He decided to heed Parsons's warning.

Long after Phil had undressed and turned off the lights and gotten into bed beside Julie, he listened for sounds from the other

CHAPTER 69

AT DAWN Phil crept into the kitchen, opened several cans of formula and poured them down the drain in the sink—it was only later he realized that if he was able to persuade Nanny to go to the store to buy more formula she'd probably take Harry with her, thus depriving him of the opportunity he sought. Then he removed the heavy desk from in front of the door.

A few hours later Phil found Nanny in the kitchen. She appeared to be going about her normal routine just as though she'd not been fired. Phil decided to go along with the pretext that she was still working for them.

"Nanny, we appear to be low on formula," he said. "I'm concerned that we might run out. With all this snow there might be shortages at the supermarket soon. Perhaps you could go out later today and pick up a few cans of it."

Nanny chuckled.

"You find my suggestion amusing?" he said.

"Quite."

"And why would that be?"

"If you're that concerned about the shortage of formula, Mr. Pressman," she said, "then why on earth would you have punctured so many tins and poured them down the drain?"

"Why would I have done *what?*" he said, but he realized he'd lost this round as well.

Julie was nearly comatose all day. Phil prowled the apartment, waiting for an opportunity to grab Harry and Julie and leave, but none presented itself.

After Nanny finished bathing Harry that evening she dressed him in his stretchie, fed him his bottle and put him to bed. Phil walked casually back into his and Julie's bedroom and began laying out Julie's warm clothing.

Nanny usually had her shower around 8 p.m. every evening. It was now 7:40. While she was in the shower might be an excellent opportunity to take Harry and try to get away.

Phil helped Julie dress—a laborious process, given her present ability to cooperate. Then he put on warm clothes himself and began to wait.

Nanny went into the kitchen and leisurely emptied the dishwasher of all the plates and glasses and cups and bowls and baby bottles and nipples and put them away in the cabinets above the sink. Then she collected all the dirty dishes, rinsed them thoroughly with the dish squeegee and loaded them into the dishwasher. Then she scoured the sink and the counter and stove. Then she mixed up the last of the baby's formula and put a pot of nipples and pacifiers on the stove to boil.

At 8:05 Nanny left the kitchen and went into her bathroom and closed the door. A moment later Phil heard the shower being turned on. It seemed to him the shower had been turned on almost immediately after Nanny closed the door. He wondered if it was too soon for her to have gotten undressed. Perhaps she'd anticipated his attempts to leave again, and only turned on the shower to lull him into thinking she was no longer wary.

He waited, using up precious moments. Satisfied she really was in the shower, he slipped out of his bedroom and down the hall into Harry's room. His hand crept along the wall to the light switch and prepared to turn it on, fully expecting to see Nanny in the chair again. But when he turned on the night-light the chair beside the bed was empty. Thank God!

Heart pounding, Phil bent over the cradle. With a silent prayer to Harry not to cry, he picked the baby up in his arms, wrapped a woolen blanket around him and quietly exited the room. Harry's eyes fluttered open but, miraculously, he did not cry.

Thank you, Harry, he said silently, and crept past the bathroom door where Nanny was still apparently showering and entered the master bedroom. Julie was sitting on the edge of their bed, fully clothed, just as he had left her.

"We're going now, honey," he whispered to her. "Are you ready?"

Not waiting for an answer, he put his free arm under hers and helped her stand up and walk out of the bedroom and through the living-dining room and up to the front door. Harry began to cry.

Oh no, he thought, please, no! He swiftly unlocked the locks on the front door, and then, to his intense disappointment, he heard the shower being turned off.

CHAPTER 70

HARRY continued to cry. Phil opened the front door and, carrying the baby in one arm and propping Julie up as best he could with the other, made his way down the hallway to the small self-service elevator. Please let the elevator be there, he prayed. Please just let it be there.

They reached the elevator and Phil pressed the button. Mercifully, the door slid open. Even before it was fully open, Phil was wedging himself and the baby and Julie inside it.

Phil pressed the first floor button, and the elevator jolted into motion.

The motion of the elevator appeared to distract Harry enough to keep him from crying, but when they alighted at the first floor he began to scream. Phil helped Julie to the outside door. As it opened, a blast of frigid air and snow almost knocked them over.

Draping the blanket over Harry's face and hoping he had enough air to breathe, Phil made his way through the snowdrifts and into the street, dragging Julie, who kept stumbling and had to be repeatedly pulled back onto her feet.

The snowfall had become a blizzard. There were no cabs on the block, no passenger cars even. Phil towed Julie down Perry Street toward Twelfth Avenue, the exceptionally wide boulevard where huge tractor-trailers thundered past at high speeds at all hours of the day and night. He kept looking back nervously over his shoulder, afraid he'd see Nanny emerge from their building.

The baby had temporarily ceased crying, perhaps intrigued by the blizzard. Julie was barely able to walk, but she continued to stumble after him, leaning on his free arm. All sounds were muffled in the thick falling snow. It was like being inside a bad head cold.

As they reached Twelfth Avenue, Phil's worst fears materialized—Nanny, in her hastily donned black overcoat, had emerged from their building and was even now heading up the street in their direction.

Phil waded out into the middle of Twelfth Avenue, looking frantically around for cabs. A passenger car hurtled toward them. Phil signaled wildly for it to stop, but it whizzed past them, spraying them with rapidly graying slush. Phil looked back over his shoulder. Nanny was now no more than a block away.

Another passenger car hurtled past them, showering them with melted snow and road grime, ignoring Phil's desperate signals to stop. Nanny was now no more than a half block away.

A sixteen-wheeler, going at least fifty, raced toward them. Phil saw it as their last chance. He suddenly thrust Harry into Julie's arms, praying her natural protective instincts would keep her upright and hanging on, and lurched directly into the path of the oncoming tractor-trailer.

The driver blasted his air horn, hit his air brakes, swerved, skidded and screeched to a stop inches from Phil's body. Phil grabbed Harry back and held him up so that the extravagantly cursing truck driver could see him.

"Our baby is sick!" Phil shouted, having decided that only a health emergency could justify his actions. "We need a ride to the hospital!"

Nanny had almost arrived at the corner.

Phil reached up and yanked open the passenger's door of the truck cab.

"Our baby is sick and so is my wife!" he said. "If you don't drive us to the hospital, they'll die!"

The driver looked down at Phil, opted to swallow his fury and motioned for them to get in. Phil handed Harry up to the driver, pulled Julie into the cab beside him and slammed the door shut, just as Nanny ran up and began to shout.

"Get going!" said Phil. "Please get going!"

Nanny pounded on the window.

"Who the hell is *that?*" said the driver, inclining his head in Nanny's direction.

"Nobody," said Phil.

"Nobody?" said the driver.

"A crazy woman who lives on our block, O.K.?" said Phil. "Get going, *please!*"

CHAPTER 71

THE DRIVER put the truck in gear. Phil looked back at Nanny, who had started getting smaller and smaller in the rearview mirror, and he began breathing a bit more easily.

"What's the closest hospital?" said the driver, a thickset man about Phil's age, wearing a greasy down vest, a denim jacket, a baseball cap and a two- or three-day growth of beard.

"Probably St. Vincent's," said Phil. "That's at Seventh Avenue and Eleventh Street."

The driver nodded and glanced uneasily at Julie and the baby.

"What's wrong with them?" he said, apparently worried he'd catch it.

"I don't know," said Phil. "I wish to God I did."

The driver continued to drive. The snow pelted the windshield as the gigantic wipers wiped it away. The Peterbilt truck's cab was high and the truck's engine was powerful, and Phil felt momentarily safe from whatever he was fleeing in Nanny.

When the driver dropped them at St. Vincent's, he became unexpectedly solicitous, helping Julie out of the truck and into the hospital, insisting on carrying the baby himself and expressing heartfelt wishes for their speedy recovery.

Phil thanked him profusely, Julie grunted, and the driver swung back up into the cab of his tractor-trailer and drove away.

Phil felt temporarily safe in the hospital. Julie, if she had been conscious, would probably say it was the proximity of all those doctor/father figures. In any case, a hospital wasn't one of the first ten places Nanny was apt to come looking for them. As long as we're here, Phil thought, we might as well find out if there's a medical basis for Julie's symptoms.

When Phil and Julie were called, a small East Indian man in

a white coat led them to a bed in the large receiving room and pulled a curtain around them.

The Indian doctor was slender and dark and his singsong voice was a parody of the Indian accents used by Mel Brooks and Robin Williams. The Indian appeared irritated at Harry's crying. Phil explained that Harry had colic, and the doctor shrugged.

"Your baby is merely fatigued, sir," said the doctor. "Take him home, put him to bed and permit him to sleep. He will recuperate considerably if you will permit him to sleep."

The doctor examined Julie. He looked in her eyes and ears and mouth, he listened to her heart through a stethoscope, he took her pulse at several locations and raised his eyebrows.

"Your wife is a runner, sir?" he said.

"No," said Phil. "Why do you ask?"

"Very good resting heart rate," said the doctor.

"What is it?" said Phil.

"Thirty-three," said the doctor.

"*Thirty-three?*" said Phil. "Her normal pulse is something like seventy-two!"

"Oh no," said the doctor, "you must be mistaken, sir. It could not go this low if it were normally seventy-two."

"Unless she were terribly sick," said Phil.

"Oh no," said the doctor, "your wife is not sick, sir. She has an excellent resting heart rate, excellent. She is merely fatigued. Take her home, put her to bed and permit her to sleep."

Phil didn't know where to go. He went to the pay phone in the lobby of the waiting room and called Mary Margaret Sullivan. She picked up on the third ring.

"I wonder if I could ask you a really crazy favor," said Phil.

"Yes?" said Sullivan.

"I'm having a kind of emergency, and I wondered if I could bring my wife and baby over to your house for a while."

"What's wrong?" said Sullivan.

"Well," said Phil, eyeing the people on the benches who were gazing interestedly in his direction, "it's a little hard to explain over the phone. I wonder if I could come over and talk to you about it."

"When would you like to come?"

"How about right now?" said Phil.

"Now would be fine," said Sullivan.

"Thank you," said Phil.

He hung up the phone and shepherded Julie and the baby out of the hospital and into a waiting cab, and gave the Libyan cabdriver Mary Margaret Sullivan's address on Central Park West.

CHAPTER 72

THE CAB sped up Eighth Avenue in the snow, swerving alarmingly, going far too fast for the condition of the unplowed streets.

"Could you slow down a little, please?" Phil called through the dirty Plexiglas partition. "We have an infant back here!"

But the Libyan either didn't hear or chose to pretend he didn't. Phil wondered what standards you had to pass to become a New York cabdriver these days and whether anybody had ever failed in the history of the test. Then he began to wonder about Nanny.

So she'd lost this round—that didn't mean she would give up. Surely she'd try to follow them. He wondered if she'd guess Phil might take them to Sullivan's apartment. Phil remembered discussing Sullivan with Nanny and telling her he felt the elderly woman was one of the few people in New York he could trust. Would she remember that?

It was a definite possibility. In fact, Nanny might even be there now—they might roll up at Sullivan's and find Nanny there waiting for them!

No, Sullivan's place was too dangerous. Where could they go, then? To Ralph Roberts's apartment. No, he'd talked about Roberts, too—Nanny would probably go there as well. But Roberts had mentioned a house he owned on eastern Long Island. Maybe Phil could ask to borrow that for a few days.

"Driver, I'm changing our destination," Phil called through the partition.

The cab did not slow.

"Driver? Hello?"

No response.

"Driver, *stop the cab!*"

Without lowering his reckless rate of speed, the driver turned around to look at Phil.

"Did you hear me?" said Phil. "I want you to stop the cab. I want to change our destination."

"Change?"

"Yes!"

Although speaking English appeared to be even more elusive a skill to the Libyan than that of driving, Phil somehow managed to direct the fellow to a phone booth. Phil located Ralph Roberts's number through Information and dialed it as the snow stung his face. Please be home, Phil prayed, please be home.

The line was answered.

"Hi, this is Ralph . . ." said the voice at the other end.

"Ralph!" said Phil gratefully. "God am I glad to hear your—"

". . . If you're a robber and you think I'm out, I should warn you that I'm sitting here in the dark with two snarling Dobermans and a double-barreled shotgun. If you're not a robber," the voice continued, "please leave your name and telephone number and the time you called after the beep, and I'll get back to you."

Phil wondered what sort of message he could leave, then he heard the beep.

"Uh, Ralph, this is Phil Pressman," he said. "It's about 10 p.m.

and I don't really know where you can reach me, because . . ."

"Pressman?"

"Ralph, you *are* there!" said Phil delightedly. "Thank God!"

"What's up?" said Roberts.

The voice sounded flat, distant, not the voice you wanted to be asking what Phil was about to ask.

"Ralph, I am calling to ask you a tremendous favor."

"Yeah . . ."

"I remember your telling me about a house you own on Long Island. In East Hampton, I think . . ."

"Yeah . . ."

"Uh, the thing is, Ralph," said Phil, wishing that Roberts would make it easier, "I've gotten myself into a bit of a bind, and I wonder if it would be at all possible for me to have access to your house on Long Island for a few days. I know it's a terrific imposition, but—"

"For a few days?" said Roberts.

"Yes," said Phil, suddenly ashamed to be asking, knowing he'd overstepped himself, knowing that Roberts was going to turn him down, but knowing that it really was an emergency and it was something he'd had to try. "Do you think that would be possible, Ralph?"

"When did you want to go out there?" said Roberts cautiously. "This weekend or what?"

"No no, now," said Phil. "Right now. Tonight."

"Tonight?"

"Yes," said Phil. "I can't really explain, but it has to do with Luci Redman and it's something of an emergency."

"With Luci Redman, eh?" said Roberts, suddenly coming to life, his voice taking on a lewd and oily pitch. "I think I know what kind of emergency you mean."

"It's not what you think," said Phil, realizing what Roberts must be imagining and then figuring the hell with it, maybe that would make him agreeable.

"Whatever you say, kid," said Roberts.

"So what do you think?" said Phil. "You think you might see your way clear to letting us have it for a few days?"

"Us, eh?" said Roberts. "Sure, you can have it—you old dog, you!"

Roberts gave him driving directions out to the house, which Phil scribbled down on a piece of paper, his fingers going numb with cold.

"The kitchen door in the back should be unlocked. The heat and water and electricity should all be working, although the house will be pretty cold when you first get there. But you ought to be able to get it hot pretty fast," Roberts added with a salacious chuckle.

"I can't tell you how grateful I am for this," said Phil.

"Don't mention it," said Roberts.

"I have to ask that you promise me one thing, though," said Phil.

"What's that?"

"Whatever you do," said Phil, "*please* don't tell anybody where we are."

"You don't have to worry about *that*," said Roberts with another lewd laugh. "My lips are sealed."

Phil next called Information for the location of the closest car rental agency open at this hour, and through no fault of the Libyan cabdriver, they actually succeeded in getting there.

The Avis rental office was manned by an alarmingly thin, pockmarked Hispanic man with a sparse beard and a mysteriously jolly disposition. Phil rented the only four-wheel vehicle available, a Jeep Cherokee, and had to pay extra for an infant seat. The jolly Hispanic man had for some reason decided that Phil and Julie were off on a skiing holiday, despite their lack of skiing gear.

"You going up to Killington?" said the rental agent, trying to fit the seatbelt through the back of the infant seat.

"No," said Phil, "not Killington."

"Pretty good skiing in Killington," said the man. "Although, I got to be honest with you, Eastern skiing is a little icy for my taste."

"Is that right," said Phil.

The rental agent was having a lot of difficulty installing the infant seat in the car.

"Yeah," said the agent. "Personally, I prefer Western skiing myself."

"Uh huh," said Phil, anxious to be under way and wishing the guy knew how to install the seat.

"I got me a time-share on a sweet little condo in Vail," said the agent. "Right there in Lion's Head. Right near the lift there. You know Vail at all?"

"Not at all," said Phil.

"I'm basically a powder skier myself," said the man. "I basically ski the back bowls."

"You don't say," said Phil.

The guy finally managed to install the seat properly and they strapped Harry into it. Then he showed Phil how to throw the car into four-wheel drive. Phil helped Julie into the car.

"Your wife looks a little tired," he said.

"She's had a hard day," said Phil.

"I wouldn't let her out on the slopes too long the first day," said the man. "The altitude, you know."

"O.K.," said Phil, starting up the engine, "thanks for the tip."

"Well, have fun," said the Hispanic man. "And remember, 'No Guts, No Glory.'"

"I'll try to remember that," said Phil, and put the Jeep in gear and set off for the Long Island Expressway.

CHAPTER 73

MARY MARGARET SULLIVAN sat at her typewriter, gazing out at the snow swirling around the balcony of her penthouse, working on the agency's pitch to a prospective client in the automotive industry and thinking about Phil Pressman.

She couldn't imagine why Pressman was bringing his wife and baby over to her apartment, but he'd seemed really upset, and this visit would give her an opportunity to at least meet the rest of his family. She liked the eccentric copywriter, despite his neuroses. She found him bright, earnest and very touching. She also found him quite amusing, even when it wasn't intentional.

Her late husband Hy had been amusing, too, but it was always intentional. Hy and Pressman were both Jewish, both talented admen, but they had nothing else even remotely in common. She wondered why she felt so fond of Pressman.

It was her impression that sons tried to be the opposite of their fathers. If she and Hy had had a son he might have been like Pressman.

The house phone buzzed. She picked it up.

"Yes, Otto?" she said.

"Miss Sullivan," said the doorman with the faintest of Germanic accents, "you have a visitor here."

"Just one?" said Mary Margaret, having expected Phil, his wife and baby.

"Yes," said the doorman. "Shall I send her up?"

"*Her?*" she said.

"Your daughter-in-law," said the doorman.

Mary Margaret frowned.

"I don't *have* a daughter-in-law," she said. "What did she say her name was?"

"It's a Miss Redman, ma'am," said the doorman.

"Miss Redman is not my daughter-in-law," she said. "If the lady wishes to see me, tell her she may phone my office for an appointment in the morning."

There was apparently some discussion between the doorman and the visitor, and then the doorman returned to the phone.

"She says it's terribly important that she comes up to see you," said Otto. "She says there is a family crisis which she must discuss with you."

"Tell Miss Redman that I don't have a daughter-in-law, Otto," she said. "And tell her that I do not wish to see her."

"Certainly, Miss Sullivan," said Otto.

She hung up the house phone. She didn't know why the Pressmans' nanny had come here, but she didn't like the sound of it and wanted to hear from Pressman himself what the emergency was before she talked to her.

She tried to concentrate on her pitch letter, but her thoughts kept drifting back to Pressman, his wife, the baby and Luci Redman. She was a little shaken at Luci Redman's appearance downstairs in her building. She didn't know why, but for some reason it seemed ominous.

She listened to the wind howling outside on the balcony, and then she got up to make herself a cup of coffee. She filled the kettle and turned on the burner, but as soon as she put the water on to boil she thought she heard a knock at the front door.

That was odd. Could Luci Redman have convinced Otto she really was Mary Margaret's daughter-in-law? Or was it Otto himself, come to plead Luci Redman's case? Mary Margaret walked to the front door and peered through the peephole.

It was Nanny.

"Miss Sullivan," said Nanny, "I have to speak to you."

How did she know I came to the door, thought Mary Margaret idly—I never said a word.

"Miss Sullivan, please open the door," said Nanny. "I have to speak with you."

"I have nothing to say to you," said Mary Margaret.

"Then let me speak to Mr. Pressman," said Nanny.

"Mr. Pressman isn't here," said Mary Margaret, wondering how she knew he was on his way.

There was temporary silence from the other side of the door, during which the kettle began to whistle.

"I wish you would tell Mr. Pressman that he is making a dreadful mistake," said Nanny. "I wish you would tell him that if he and Mrs. Pressman and the child return to the apartment immediately the mistake can be rectified. I wish you would tell him that. Will you please tell him that?"

Mary Margaret found the whistling of the kettle particularly grating because she was suddenly afraid.

"I just *told* you," said Mary Margaret. "Mr. Pressman is not here. And now, if you'll excuse me, I must return to my work."

"I cannot leave without speaking personally to Mr. Pressman," said Nanny.

"Then stay there as long as you like," said Mary Margaret. "And I'm going to telephone the police."

She went to the phone and dialed her local precinct.

"This is Mary Margaret Sullivan," she said. "I live in the penthouse of the San Sebastian Towers and I have a prowler whom I believe to be armed and dangerous. I need you to send someone over here as fast as you can."

The desk sergeant checked Mary Margaret's address and assured her that a radio car would be dispatched immediately. She breathed a sigh of relief.

A long twenty minutes passed, during which time she could find nothing to do but drink coffee and listen to the howling of the wind, and then she heard a loud knocking at the door.

"Who is it?" she called, not anxious to get too close to the door if Luci Redman was still on the other side of it.

"Police, Miss Sullivan!"

Mary Margaret advanced to the door and looked through the

peephole. There were indeed two uniformed patrolmen outside, and no sign at all of Luci Redman. She unlocked her several locks and let the policemen into the apartment.

"You reported a prowler?" said the taller of the two cops.

"Yes," she said. "Did you see anybody on the way up?"

"No, ma'am. What did he look like?"

"It wasn't a he, it was a she," said Mary Margaret.

"Are you acquainted with the prowler?"

"No," she said.

"Can you tell us what she was doing here?"

"She was looking for someone she believes to be here who isn't," she said. "She said she wasn't going to leave until I let her in to talk to him."

"And what leads you to suspect that she is dangerous?"

"I . . . just had a feeling, is all," she said.

"Yes, ma'am."

She saw the look that passed between the two policemen and knew that they had written her off as a crazy old lady who imagined things. They made a show of looking perfunctorily around the apartment, and then they left.

When they had gone, Mary Margaret triple-locked the front door again and returned to the kitchen to make more coffee. Something was bothering her, and for the moment she was unable to put her finger on it. Something about the arrival of the police.

And then she had it. The police had just come right upstairs. Otto hadn't announced them on the house phone as he normally did. Otto was quite conscientious about not letting people go upstairs unannounced. Why had he not announced the policemen?

She thought she heard a noise in the bedroom. Perhaps it was one of the shutters banging against the bedroom window. She'd have to fix it before she went to bed or the banging would keep her up all night. Then she heard the noise again and feared the window itself might be banging.

Carrying her steaming cup of coffee, she walked into the bedroom and was upset to see that the window had indeed blown open and a good deal of snow had come into the room and covered the carpeting.

And then she looked up and realized that the snow was not the only thing that had come in from the terrace.

CHAPTER 74

THERE WERE understandably few cars on the Long Island Expressway. There was so much snow on the unplowed highway that it was impossible to see where the shoulders of the road were. It looked to Phil as though he were driving on a limitless white plain, on a glacier up at the North Pole. And the pattern of snowflakes, lit by the Jeep's headlights and flying straight at the windshield, looked like the special effect on *Star Trek* when the Starship Enterprise went into hyperspace.

The Jeep's four-wheel drive kept the vehicle steady in the snow, and its progress was peaceful, surreal and in slow motion. Even when the occasional car ahead of the Jeep went out of control and did a three-sixty, it was in slow motion, which added to the dream-like effect.

After the first hour of driving, Harry began to cry in a way that Phil had come to know as his hungry cry. Phil got off the expressway at the next exit and drove till he found an all-night grocery store.

Leaving Julie in the car with Harry, he went in and tried to find formula, diapers and baby bottles. The store did have disposable diapers, although they were Pampers and not the Luvs which Phil preferred, but formula and baby bottles were nowhere in evidence. The teenaged boy at the cash register thought the 7-Eleven at the next exit might have what Phil sought.

Phil got back into the car. Harry was now crying furiously. The 7-Eleven at the next exit had baby bottles and nipples but no formula. Phil bought the bottles and the nipples and some food for himself and Julie, and although he knew Harry was too young for cow's milk, he bought some anyway and then got back in the Jeep.

The next three exits had no stores that were open, and Harry was now hysterical. Phil was getting desperate. He wondered if he could get away with feeding Harry ordinary milk. He asked Julie what she thought, but she had sunk back into whatever she was in before. If only he could talk to Sullivan, she might know. He really should have called her to tell her what they were doing and to get further advice from her.

He went to the phone in the grocery store and dialed Sullivan's number. The line was answered by her machine. That's strange, he thought, she told me she works very late at night. Well, not tonight, apparently.

CHAPTER 75

MARY MARGARET SULLIVAN and Nanny stood looking at each other in silence.

"I told you I was not going to leave until I spoke to Mr. Pressman," said Nanny.

"And I told you he isn't here," said Mary Margaret.

Nanny brushed past her, shaking the snow off her coat and boots, and made a cursory search of the apartment.

"Where did you send them?" said Nanny calmly.

"I didn't send them anywhere," said Mary Margaret.

"Where did they go?"

"I told you, I don't know."

Nanny regarded Mary Margaret impassively for a moment, then, without warning, struck her in the chest so hard that Mary Margaret caved in and sank to the floor.

"Where?" said Nanny.

Looking up at Nanny standing over her, Mary Margaret found it hard to catch her breath.

"Where?" said Nanny.

Mary Margaret weakly shook her head. She was in trouble, in the worst trouble of her life, and for once she couldn't think of a way out.

"I can wait," said Nanny. "I've got all the time in the world, and then some."

"What . . . do you . . . want with them?" said Mary Margaret with great difficulty. Her chest ached frighteningly and she could scarcely breathe.

"I am the baby's nanny," said Nanny. "I simply want to do my job."

The phone began to ring. Then they heard Mary Margaret's voice speaking from the answering machine, asking the caller to leave a message after the beep.

"Hi, it's Phil Pressman," said the caller.

Both women turned to look at the phone. Please don't tell us where you are or where you're going, thought Mary Margaret.

"I just wanted to tell you that we're all right," Pressman's voice continued. "I changed my mind about coming over and I wanted to ask you some advice, but I guess I'll have to try you again when you're actually there. We're headed . . . ."

"No!" thought Mary Margaret, and then realized she had said it aloud.

But apparently Pressman had reservations about telling even an answering machine where they were headed, because he let the thought trickle out.

"I'll call you later," said Pressman finally, and the line clicked off.

Mary Margaret lay on the floor, trying to think what to do. It was now obvious to her that she was dealing with a dangerous psychotic. It was, she realized, altogether possible that she might not survive Luci Redman's visit unless she could come up with something ingenious and fast. Several dozen possible solutions raced through her mind in high-speed montage and were summarily rejected.

"Mr. Pressman said, 'We're headed . . . ,'" said Luci Redman. "Where is it they are headed?"

"Do you honestly think I would tell you that, even if I knew?" said Mary Margaret.

"I think that you would," said Luci Redman, "in time."

"I ask you to leave this apartment immediately," said Mary Margaret, stretching her hand out along the carpet to grab the leg of a chair to pull herself up, "before you get into further trouble."

"It is not I who am in trouble, dear," said Luci Redman, stepping on Mary Margaret's hand.

CHAPTER 76

PHIL gave up on finding formula, poured milk from the carton he bought into one of the new baby bottles, spilling a fair amount of it on the floor of the Jeep in the process, and gave the bottle to Harry. The baby seemed slightly confused at first, but then sucked at it voraciously. Phil hoped Harry could digest it. Julie dozed in her twilight world.

Phil got back on the Long Island Expressway. The blizzard continued. The snowflakes, lit by the headlights and blowing directly into the windshield, were beginning to have a psychedelic, hypnotic effect on him. Once or twice he found himself drifting into a twilight world of his own and had to shake his head vigorously to remain awake. He couldn't afford to fall asleep at the wheel.

At Exit 70 Phil left the expressway and picked up Route 111. If there had been few cars on the expressway, there were fewer still on Route 111. Roberts's directions indicated they were now more than two-thirds of the way to the house. Harry, having drained the bottle, was asleep at last in his infant seat. Julie looked more dead than alive.

Phil realized he was practically sleep-driving. He pulled up at the Gateway Diner on Route 111, hurried in and ordered two cups of coffee to go. A middle-aged truck driver was sitting at the counter, trying to make time with the young blonde waitress.

"Boy, some night out there, huh?" said the waitress to Phil, writing up his check and then impaling it on a wicked-looking spindle.

"Sure is," said Phil.

"We're supposed to get another six inches tonight," said the waitress.

"*I'll* give you six inches tonight, honey," said the trucker.

"Don't you wish," said the waitress. "I don't even know if I'm going to be able to get home tonight."

"If not, you can stay with *me*," said the trucker.

"Don't you wish," said the waitress.

Phil returned to the Jeep and drank both coffees there. The heat of the coffee steamed up Phil's glasses. In the short time it took to sit and drink the two cups, the windshield got completely coated with a blanket of white.

Phil put the car in gear again. Route 111 ran directly into the Sunrise Highway, a four-lane divided pavement. The farther Phil got from New York, the safer he felt. There was no conceivable way that Nanny could follow them out here, he thought. If that were true, then why was he so jumpy?

Roberts had been terrific to lend them his house. And Mary Margaret Sullivan had been great, too. Phil was extremely touched at the elderly woman's warmth and level of caring. She was, he felt, his first real friend in New York. When all of this was over he wanted to find some way to express his gratitude to her. He found himself wondering suddenly how much longer she would live.

CHAPTER 77

IN THE LITTLE ROOM just off the main lobby of the San Sebastian Towers, on a worn brown leatherette chair with a rip in its seat through which a thick yellow piece of polyurethane foam protruded, sat Otto Montag the doorman.

Otto Montag wore a black doorman's uniform with gold braid on the sleeves and on the epaulets. He wore a white wing collar and a black bow tie and a black officer's cap with a patent leather brim and more gold braid and the crest of the San Sebastian Towers on the front of it.

An old black and white Motorola TV set sat on a desk scarcely three feet away from Otto Montag. The set was a tenant discard, so it sputtered and the picture occasionally rolled.

The set was tuned to a rerun of *The David Susskind Show*. Among the panelists were George Segal, David Steinberg and Mel Brooks. You could tell it was a very old show because of how everybody was dressed. Some of the panelists were wearing leather. All of them had rather long sideburns.

Mel Brooks had totally taken over the show. Susskind, trying to regain the helm, framed a multi-claused question to Brooks full of polysyllabic words, in the middle of which Brooks cut him off with, "Oh, shut up, dummy!"

The audience, and Susskind himself, to his credit, erupted in laughter. Otto Montag did not laugh. He sat staring straight ahead, looking not at the screen but at a point on the wall two feet beyond it. His eyes were glazed. His head lolled at a disquieting angle.

CHAPTER 78

HERE WERE Mary Margaret's options: Hanging loosely on the wall of the living room was an antique samurai sword which she'd bought in Japan. On the kitchen counter, stuck in a butcher block cube like Excalibur, were several extremely sharp knives and a meat cleaver with an edge stropped fine enough to split hairs.

Any one of these, were Mary Margaret able to wrap her fingers around it before Nanny stopped her, could prove to be her salvation. The trick was not to have it used against her.

"Where did they go?" said Nanny again.

Nanny didn't appear to be in a particular hurry for the answer. She seemed confident that she would learn what she wanted to know in time.

"Let me ask you something," said Mary Margaret.

"Yes."

"Assuming that I *did* know where they went . . ."

"Yes . . ."

"And assuming that I told you . . ."

"Yes . . ."

"What would you do with the information?"

"I would go and bring them back home where they belong."

"And you wouldn't harm them?"

"Miss Sullivan, why would I harm them? I am their nanny. It is my job to take care of them."

"How do I know that you're telling the truth?"

"I give you my word as a professional and as an Englishwoman."

Mary Margaret considered this.

"Very well," she said. "Help me up."

"Are you willing to tell me where they are?"

"First help me up," said Mary Margaret.

Nanny assisted Mary Margaret to her feet.

"Thank you," said Mary Margaret.

"Are you all right?" said Nanny.

"I think so," said Mary Margaret. "I think you knocked the wind out of me, that's all."

"You think I what?" said Nanny.

"Knocked the wind out of me when you hit me."

Nanny stared at her.

"I didn't hit you," said Nanny. "You tripped and fell."

"I tripped and fell?" said Mary Margaret.

"Yes," said Nanny.

Nanny continued to stare.

"Perhaps you're right," said Mary Margaret. "Perhaps I tripped and fell."

"Would you like to tell me now where they went?" said Nanny.

"Provided I can find it," said Mary Margaret.

"Provided you can find what?"

"The slip of paper I wrote it down on when Mr. Pressman phoned me before you arrived."

"Ah," said Nanny. "Which telephone were you using at the time?"

A choice now, thought Mary Margaret, this is where I have to make a choice—the sword in the living room or the knives and the cleaver in the kitchen.

"The one in the kitchen," said Mary Margaret.

"Good," said Nanny. "Let's go into the kitchen, then, shall we?"

Nanny followed Mary Margaret into the kitchen. On the counter, under the wall-mounted telephone, just to the left of the block containing the knives and the cleaver, was a yellow notepad with pencil scribbles on it. It was entirely believable, from a distance of greater than three feet, that one of those scribbles was an address that Pressman had given Mary Margaret on the phone before Nanny arrived.

"Would you care for a cup of tea first?" said Mary Margaret.

"Oh no, thank you," said Nanny.

"You're quite sure?" said Mary Margaret. "I have some nice English Breakfast tea, if you'd like it, and also some Earl Grey."

"Oh no, not now, thanks," said Nanny. "Maybe afterwards."

The trick here, Mary Margaret thought, was not going to be getting to the block. The trick was going to be grabbing whichever of the blades in the block would be the most expedient to use, withdrawing it from the block and embedding it in the least amount of time in whichever part of Nanny's anatomy that would do the most damage.

Time was of the essence here, thought Mary Margaret, and she was interested to see that time had, in fact, cranked down to almost one-third normal speed. This was, she realized, a classic reaction to panic, the feeling that time was slowing down, and yet she didn't feel panicked, she felt exhilarated. Exhilarated and strangely calm.

"Where is the address?" said Nanny.

"Over there on the pad under the phone," said Mary Margaret. "I'd better read it to you, though—I'm afraid my handwriting is atrocious."

The question of which blade would be the most expedient to use was now obvious to Mary Margaret—the cleaver was clearly the sharpest edge in the house and would surely inflict the greatest damage.

"I suppose that's why I use a typewriter," said Mary Margaret.

"Excuse me?" said Nanny.

"I said I suppose that's why I use a typewriter," said Mary Margaret. "Because of my atrocious handwriting."

"Ah yes. Quite," said Nanny.

The question of how to use the cleaver deserved a bit more thought. She would grip it in her right hand, of course, because she was right-handed. And she would have to make one upward motion to clear it from the block and get it high enough above her head to put some power behind it. And then she'd have to make a second motion to bring it out in front of her and downward as close to the intersection of Nanny's neck and right shoulder as possible.

Just two quick, clean motions—one upward, and one downward—should do the trick, she thought.

She would have to pivot to the left, of course, on her left foot, to face Nanny during the motion of withdrawing the cleaver and raising it above her head, because to pivot on the downward motion would deflect too much energy away from embedding the blade in Nanny's neck.

"Shall I get it or shall you?" said Nanny.

"No no, allow *me*," said Mary Margaret, and stepped to the counter. She reached for the yellow pad with her left hand and let her right hand close around the handle of the meat cleaver.

CHAPTER 79

AFTER TWENTY MINUTES OF DRIVING, the Sunrise Highway turned from four lanes to two, although with all the snow on the ground it was hard to tell. At the Southampton bypass, Phil headed left on Route 27 toward East Hampton.

Forty-five minutes later, at the intersection of North Main and Cedar Street in East Hampton, Phil turned left again and headed into the Northwest Woods. The drifts got higher as Phil turned off on Sleepy Pond Drive, and he followed that to Live Oak Road. The drifts on Live Oak Road were so high that even the four-wheel-drive Jeep had trouble getting through.

No houses were visible from the street, only dense woods. The sign at the mouth of the driveway said "Roberts." The driveway itself was more than a block in length and flanked by cedar forest and barely wide enough for the car to pass. Several times the Jeep stalled in the heavy drifts, and Phil had to rock the car back and forth to get it going again.

At the end of the driveway was the house. Phil pulled in as close as possible and set the emergency brake. Leaving the headlights on and the engine and heater running, he got out of the car.

He waded through the thigh-high drifts and began walking around the far side of the house to get to the kitchen door in the back. The house was low and modern, and appeared to have floor-to-ceiling windows and sliding glass doors in most of the rooms.

Although Phil was under the impression that Ralph often used the house in winter, someone had draped sheets over the couches in the living room, which gave the place an eerie look. Sheets, he thought, were what you threw over corpses, and then he brushed the thought away.

Although he had never seen it before, Phil felt there was something oddly familiar about the house. And then he knew what it

175

was—it was the house in his dream, the dream where the monster from the forest broke in and attacked Harry.

As Phil made his way around the house he heard the deep snow creak under his boots. He stopped to listen. It was so quiet he could hear individual snowflakes strike the surface of his coat.

The tall cedar trees sagged under the weight of the unusually heavy snowfall. The forest, Phil noted, came within five feet of the house on all sides. It was as if the trees were poised, waiting to swallow up the house entirely.

That is a crazy image, he thought. This is a marvelous house in a marvelous, peaceful wooded area, and if I ever have the money to own a weekend house, I would want one just like this, although perhaps I wouldn't be very anxious to stay there alone.

As Phil reached the back door he thought he saw something large slip through the trees just at the edge of his field of vision. He wondered what it could have been. Maybe a deer. Maybe a dog. Maybe a wolf—were there wolves in the woods of Long Island?

Not too likely. But he did recall reading somewhere that thoughtless seasonal residents often abandoned dogs out here at the end of the summer when they returned to the city. The sturdier dogs, the ones that survived, became wild and ran in packs. Packs of wild dogs, the article said, frequently attacked and killed for food. Phil walked the last few feet to the kitchen with his back to the house.

The back door was unlocked, just as Ralph had said it would be, but Phil had to brush away a five-foot snowdrift before he could open it. He stepped inside. The house was cold and smelled faintly of summer mold.

At first Phil had difficulty finding the lights. Trying to steer clear of the shapes draped in sheets, he finally succeeded in locating a light switch and turned on some lamps in the living room. With the lights on the place appeared less spooky.

In the big stone fireplace there was an iron grate with six cedar logs stacked inside it. In a chest against the wall he found some kindling and some yellowed copies of the Sunday *New York Times*. Phil crumpled some newspaper and stuck it and the kindling under the logs and lit a fire. Then he went back to the car for Julie and the baby.

Phil carried the baby in first. In one of the back bedrooms he found a good-sized bed. Phil put the baby down in the middle of the bed, changed his diaper, covered him with a quilted comforter and then piled cushions around him so he couldn't roll off onto the floor.

Once the baby was settled Phil went back for Julie. It was no mean feat dragging her through the snow to the house, but he was eventually able to get her into the bedroom adjacent to the one where the baby was lying. Because the house was still quite cold, Phil merely took Julie's boots off and then rolled her under the covers of the bed, fully clothed. He found a thermostat on the wall and turned it up to seventy-five.

On his final trip to the Jeep he removed all the groceries he'd bought, then locked the car up for the night. He felt sure that people in this area never locked their cars up at night, but he was a city boy and a fairly nervous one at that.

He put the perishables he'd bought into the refrigerator in the kitchen, and then he spent about ten minutes taking all the sheets off the furniture and going through every room in the house and making sure that all the doors and windows were safely locked.

There were eight sliding glass doors and twelve floor-to-ceiling windows. Phil felt exposed and vulnerable to the outside. He was aware that with the lights on anyone or anything outside could look in and see him, although he couldn't see anything outside.

He felt relatively safe in the house with all the doors and windows locked, but he wasn't happy there was so much exposed glass and so many doors. He wasn't sure what it was he wanted to defend against, but he found himself wishing he had a weapon.

There were fire tools in a rack by the side of the hearth. Those could serve as weapons. There were, he remembered, knives on a magnetic rack in the kitchen. Between fire tools and knives he had enough things with which to defend himself.

He considered lying down next to Julie in the bedroom next to the baby's and then reconsidered. There was no reason to believe that any danger might present itself tonight, but if it did, the living room, which faced the driveway, would afford him the best and earliest warning.

He went into the living room and examined the couch in front of the fireplace as a potential sleeping area, and was encouraged to find that it was a Castro convertible. He took off the cushions and pulled out the tucked section.

In a small cedar closet off the living room he located several musty-smelling sheets and old olive-drab wool blankets that looked as if they might have come from someone's military service. He carried these back into the living room and fit them loosely over the mattress.

He turned off the lights and lay down on the couch and strained his eyes in the darkness to see into the woods. He could see nothing but the trees and the snow, and after a while he permitted his eyes to close and he just lay there listening. He listened to the sound of the wind sighing in the trees and he listened to the sound of the snow softly striking the windows.

Just before he dozed off he heard something heavy brush against the exterior wall on the far side of the house.

CHAPTER 80

MOTION NUMBER ONE: Mary Margaret yanked the meat cleaver abruptly from its nest in the butcher block and hoisted it high above her head, while pivoting smoothly on her left foot.

Motion number two: She brought the cleaver out and down with all her might toward Nanny's neck. But Nanny saw the blow coming and was able to step slightly to her right as the blow descended.

The cleaver did not hit Nanny squarely at the juncture of neck and shoulder as Mary Margaret had hoped. It merely grazed Nanny's left shoulder, slicing through the heavy wool fabric of her black overcoat, the light cotton fabric of her white uniform and the outer layer of the skin of her shoulder. Blood spurted from the wound, staining both garments.

Nanny did not cry out. She made no sound at all, but took another, larger step to her right and stood absolutely still, breathing deeply and evenly, ignoring the flow of blood from her shoulder for the moment, coolly gazing at her attacker and sizing up the situation.

Mary Margaret's breathing was shallow and irregular. She knew that she had gambled and lost, that although she still held the meat cleaver, the element of surprise was gone, and with it whatever slight advantage she might have possessed, that there was now little hope she could do anything at all.

If only she had struck faster. If only she had not telegraphed her moves so that Nanny had a chance to step out of the way. If only she had been about twenty or thirty years younger.

What is she waiting for, thought Mary Margaret—why does she just stand there, looking at me?

Then Nanny reached toward the stove at her immediate right and seized a large copper-bottomed frying pan off the nearest burner.

Holding it ahead of her as a shield, she slowly advanced on the terrified, cleaver-wielding woman.

CHAPTER 81

RALPH ROBERTS was having trouble sleeping. He kept thinking about Phil Pressman driving out to his house in East Hampton with Luci Redman, kept thinking about Phil and Luci sitting before the stone hearth in the living room, hearing the flames leap and snap and hiss above the logs, kept thinking about them perhaps beginning foreplay right there, with Phil sliding his hand under her white uniform skirt and up her stockinged leg, or perhaps taking her straight to the bedroom, *Ralph's* bedroom, pulling back the sheets, *Ralph's* sheets, tearing each other's clothes off and then making raw, animalistic love. Ralph was sick with envy.

It wasn't that Ralph hadn't had his share of women in that house, because he had. A few local women—waitresses, shopgirls, even a librarian—but mostly women from the city—schoolteachers, illustrators, media buyers and secretaries in the agency with whom it had then become awkward to work in the same office afterwards. And, sadly, not one of these women had ever been as exciting in bed as he'd imagined.

The best part for him was always the anticipation. The overtures. The fantasies, the preparations, the seductions. The first kisses, the undressing, the foreplay, the beginnings of sex. After that it was pretty much downhill for him. The intercourse was always pleasant but predictable, the climaxes somewhat anticlimactic, and after that he would have been perfectly content if the women had left his bed and gone along home.

He knew that this was a churlish attitude, and so he always had them stay the night, always made perfunctory and even less satisfying love the following morning, without benefit of toothpaste or underarm deodorant, always shared an awkward breakfast and tried to make pointless conversation with them.

The longest he had ever gone with anyone was seven months, and that was with a woman who'd had another boyfriend. Ralph suspected he just wasn't the marrying kind, and he *knew* he wasn't the fathering kind. He pitied men like Phil Pressman who'd become both husbands and fathers, pitied them and, to be honest about it, envied them a little as well.

Perhaps it would have been nice to have a wife to share a life with, a child to carry on the family name, a family to huddle together with in the late winter years. Well, it still wasn't too late. If Ralph found the right woman, he might yet be persuaded to try something a little more committed.

But it would have to be the right woman. It would have to be someone strong enough to hold his interest, someone with a mind of her own, someone who was maybe even a little kinky so he didn't know in advance every single thing she was going to say and do. Somebody like . . . Well, somebody like Luci Redman.

Ralph had never met Luci Redman, of course, but from the picture on Phil's desk and the things Phil had said about her, Luci Redman sounded like the kind of gal who was almost a match for Ralph. It was pretty clear that she was too much woman for poor Phil Pressman. Maybe when Phil was through with her, Ralph would suggest an introduction.

CHAPTER 82

NANNY stood in Mary Margaret Sullivan's bathroom in her red-spattered white slip and examined the cut in her shoulder. It was really only a flesh wound, and not a very serious one at that. The initial flow of blood had been staunched by applying pressure with a dish towel for several minutes, and now it appeared to have stopped completely.

Nanny opened the medicine cabinet and examined its contents with professional interest. She took out a brown plastic bottle of hydrogen peroxide, a dark blue cardboard package of sterile gauze with little red crosses on the top, a dark blue box of sterile cotton, a roll of flesh-colored adhesive tape and a small pair of surgical scissors.

She cleansed the wound thoroughly with sterile cotton soaked in hydrogen peroxide, then made a light dressing with the gauze and adhesive tape. Then she put the gauze and the cotton back in the box, the top back on the peroxide bottle, and boxes, bottle, tape and scissors back into the cabinet. She left the bathroom and began tidying up.

She cleaned up the mess in the kitchen and then she started in on the laundry. She put the dish towel she'd used to stop the flow of blood into the sink to presoak. Then she took off her bloody uniform and put that in the sink, too. Then she noticed that there was blood on her slip and even on her brassiere, and so she removed these and put them into the sink as well.

She filled the sink with cold water and dissolved plenty of Clorox 2 all-fabric bleach in it. Leaving the clothes to soak in the kitchen sink, she went into Mary Margaret Sullivan's bedroom closet and surveyed the available garments. She selected a blue flannel robe that was turning slightly purple with age and put it on.

While her clothes were soaking she had time to browse. She

went into the living room and amused herself with the art and artifacts on the wall and the extensive library of books on the bookshelves.

After half an hour she returned to the kitchen, removed the clothes from the sink and put them into the washing machine. She collected the dirty dishes on the counter and on the kitchen table and rinsed them off in the sink. Then she stacked them neatly in the dishwasher, poured in a little Cascade, closed the dishwasher door, locked the handle and pressed the button marked Heavy Wash.

She noticed that the bottoms of the copper pans hanging up on the wall were getting dull and so she took them down and polished them with Twinkle copper cleaner.

When the washing machine buzzed she transferred the wet clothes from the washer to the drier, and then, as the drum in the drier began to revolve, she returned to the living room looking for something to do.

She found herself annoyed by the lint on the couch. She went into the service closet, got out the canister-style vacuum cleaner, and, beginning to hum to herself, vacuumed the carpet and the couch.

She enjoyed the sound of the vacuum cleaner, enjoyed seeing the hose suck up the lint and the dust, and the work went very rapidly. By the time the buzzer on the drier sounded she had vacuumed the living room, the dining room and the bedroom, had had time to wash out the bathtub, the toilet and the bathroom sink with Comet cleanser, even had time to Windex the medicine cabinet mirror and polish the chrome faucets with Soft Scrub.

She put the blue flannel robe back in the closet between the two dresses where she'd found it. Then she returned to the kitchen, removed her bra, slip and uniform from the drier and put them on.

Then she put the Twinkle back under the sink and the Clorox 2 back on the shelf above the washing machine. She put the vacuum cleaner, Comet, Windex, Soft Scrub and rags back in the service closet, turned off all the lights and left by the front door, making sure to pull it securely shut behind her.

CHAPTER 83

PHIL woke with a jolt. It was not possible to know how long he had slept. It was still night. The blizzard had spent itself, and the full moon appeared between the clouds. The reflected light of the moon on the snow was almost bright enough to read by. It looked like scenes in movies which were shot day-for-night—underexposed in full sunlight to simulate moonlight.

What had awakened Phil, he now realized, was a sound very much like somebody at the back door, trying quietly to get in. He picked up the poker from its rack beside the hearth and crept into the kitchen. He took a steak knife off the magnetic rack. Holding the poker in his left hand and the steak knife in his right, Phil flattened himself against the wall and crept crablike toward the kitchen door.

He waited, motionless, standing behind the door, poker raised over his head, holding his breath and listening, for what seemed like several minutes. When he could hold it in no longer he let his breath out. There was no sound from the other side of the kitchen door.

He crept to the window which had a view beyond the door and looked outside. There was no one and nothing to be seen, just the cedar forest in brilliant moonlight and crisp shadows on the blue-white snow.

He walked softly through the entire house and checked all eight doors and found them still locked. Then he checked Julie and Harry and found them sleeping peacefully. He took Julie's pulse. It was still thirty-three.

He returned to the living room, lay down on the convertible couch in front of the stove with the still glowing coals, closed his eyes and tried to slip back into sleep.

Harry's crying awakened Phil at first light. Phil got up off the couch, considerably more fatigued than before he'd slept, and went into the baby's room. He felt as though a tractor-trailer had run over his back. He changed Harry's diaper and carried him into the kitchen. He took the carton of milk out of the refrigerator, filled up the baby bottle and found a plastic container in which to warm it up.

When the bottle was warm Phil fed it to Harry, scanning the woods for signs of movement. Harry was content as long as he was nursing, but when he finished he resumed his crying.

Phil put Harry over his shoulder and thumped his back impatiently, hoping to release the baby's burp. Harry tried to move out of burping position into cuddling position against Phil's neck. Phil was touched by the gesture, but realized they'd both feel better if Harry burped. Phil eased Harry back over his shoulder and continued to thump his back. The burp was released but the crying continued. Phil paced swiftly around the house, bouncing Harry as roughly as he could to engage his interest. As long as the bouncing was violent, Harry remained quiet.

Phil wondered how long he was going to be able to stay here in Ralph's house in the woods, standing guard over his family and bouncing Harry. In a few hours it would be early enough to call Mary Margaret again. He needed to talk to her.

CHAPTER 84

NANNY stretched luxuriously, yawned and rolled over in Mr. and Mrs. Pressman's bed. She was wearing one of Mrs. Pressman's nightgowns and enjoyed the idea of being able to sleep in this bed at last.

She would continue to sleep here once she had brought Mr. and Mrs. Pressman and the baby back to the apartment. Mr. and Mrs. Pressman could alternate as her partners in the master bedroom, and whoever she was not sleeping with could stay in *her* old room.

What if they should refuse to return with her to the apartment? It was a possibility she'd had to consider. Well, Mrs. Pressman wasn't going to refuse to do anything at all, so long as Nanny kept her comatose. But Nanny couldn't keep her in that state indefinitely. What if, when Nanny brought her out of it, both Mr. and Mrs. Pressman refused to return to the apartment—what then?

Then Nanny would simply have to do away with the Pressmans and find herself another family, just as she had done with the Millmans, the Conroys, the Parsons and all the rest. Sad, but, unfortunately, unavoidable.

The Parsons business had been particularly unpleasant. She had never expected Mrs. Parsons to react so badly to being seduced. As if being introduced to loving another woman was so terrible. Really! She had certainly seemed to like it well enough at first. Surely there were less messy means of suicide, however. It was fortunate the baby hadn't survived the fire, judging by how badly he'd been burned. And Mrs. Parsons herself had been so brittle when the firemen found her body that she'd crumbled when they picked her up. Mr. Parsons had survived with minor burns, of course, but he was no longer much use to anybody.

It wasn't Nanny's fault. She had *tried* to keep the Parsons together as a family with herself as the cohesive center, and for a while it had actually worked—Mr. Parsons, Mrs. Parsons, the baby—they had all let Nanny take complete care of them, and all had truly grown to love her, grown to love her better than they loved each other or themselves.

There was nothing wrong with that, either. Without love as dedicated and pure as that to nourish her, Nanny would not have been able to take proper care of them, or any of the others, for that matter.

Without love as dedicated and pure as that to nourish her, Nanny herself would wither and die, as vampires were said to wither and die without the nourishment of human blood.

Death was not unknown to Nanny. In London a century and a half before, Malcolm and Diana Redman, her accursed mother and father, who never wanted a child, who never should have borne a child, who were so selfishly and all-consumingly in love with each other that they scarcely knew little Luci *existed*, practiced a form of ceremonial magic loosely based upon *The Book of Sacred Magic of Abra-Melin the Mage.*

On Luci's seventh birthday, Malcolm and Diana Redman offered her to Edward Alexander Seagrave, the high priest of their order, as a symbolic bride. The ritual consummation of the marriage on the magical altar was unexpectedly brutal. The terrified girl hemorrhaged and bled to death from internal injuries. In the twilight world Luci Redman inhabited during those final minutes of her life, she cried out to some greater power to redress this terrible injustice.

Mercifully, her prayers were answered. Seagrave, Malcolm and Diana Redman all contracted venereal disease and perished within the year, and Luci Redman was born again, given a second chance at life and at finding the only meaningful kind of love in the world.

Love. Pure, perfect, undiluted, undivided, unconditional love. Sadly, she failed to find it with her second set of parents, Michael and Emily Broderick, as well. They, like Malcolm and Diana Redman, seemed to care less for their daughter than they did for each other. Just prior to attaining the dreaded age of seven again, the little girl left the Broderick home to forage for herself in the streets of London. Because of her fierce will to live and to find love, she survived.

Someday, she knew, perfect love would be hers forever. Perfect love which recognized her as its sole object and beneficiary would satisfy her terrible hunger. The quest for that love was all-important, all-consuming. Its attainment ultimately justified anything, even killing.

Nanny showered slowly in Mr. and Mrs. Pressman's shower, taking plenty of time. She shampooed her hair with Mrs. Pressman's shampoo, then dried herself with Mr. and Mrs. Pressman's bath sheets, blew her hair dry with Mr. and Mrs. Pressman's hair drier, and massaged plenty of Mrs. Pressman's Swiss Formula moisturizer into her skin. Her skin was beginning to look wrinkled and really old. It would soon be time for something stronger than Swiss Formula.

Nanny went through Mrs. Pressman's drawers and closet to see if there was anything else of hers that she wished to wear, but decided she preferred her own things, and walked back to her former bedroom to select underwear and stockings and a fresh white uniform.

After a hearty breakfast of sausages, grilled tomatoes, eggs, toast and tea, Nanny rinsed the dishes, stacked them in the dishwasher, did a little light vacuuming and left the apartment.

The snow had stopped several hours ago, but Perry Street remained unplowed. Several people—superintendents and tenants alike—were shoveling the sidewalks in front of their buildings. Nanny walked through the high drifts to Twelfth Avenue, where she hailed a cab and gave the driver a midtown address.

She alighted at the building on Madison Avenue, took an elevator to the thirteenth floor, walked through the heavy glass doors which said Sullivan, Stouffer, Cohn and McConnell, and up to the reception desk.

"May I help you?" said the blonde British receptionist.

"You may indeed," said Nanny, pleased at the familiar accent. "Miss Luci Redman is here to see Mr. Roberts."

The receptionist smiled.

"Do you have an appointment, Miss Redman?"

"I do not," said Nanny.

"Well," said the receptionist, "Mr. Roberts sees people only by appointment, I fear."

Luci smiled.

"Just tell Mr. Roberts that Luci Redman is here, dear," she said. "He'll know."

CHAPTER 85

MARIA ESPOSITO walked up to the San Sebastian Towers promptly at 8:56 a.m. It would take her exactly four minutes to cross to the elevator, wait for it to come, then ascend to the penthouse floor. In sixteen years of cleaning for Miss Sullivan three times a week she had never missed a day due to illness and she had never been late.

Anticipating delays due to last night's blizzard, Maria had allowed a full hour and a quarter extra this morning to get to Manhattan from Brooklyn on the subway and had arrived on Central Park West exactly on schedule.

Maria was alarmed to see several police cars outside the building, and when she walked in Enrique the doorman informed her in Spanish that Otto the night man had been found dead in the little room adjoining the lobby. Enrique had not been able to get the police to tell him anything, but he suspected a heart attack.

Maria was saddened to hear of Otto's death, but she did not know the gentleman, and besides, she had no time for gossip today, so she rang for the elevator, and when it arrived she took it up to the penthouse floor. By the time she reached Miss Sullivan's door she already had her keys out, as usual, and then she turned the three locks and entered the apartment.

Miss Sullivan had been at it again, she saw, vacuuming and straightening up just as if there were no Maria Esposito coming in three days a week to clean. Maria smiled a frowning smile, shook her head and then went into the bathroom to change.

Oh no! She had done the bathroom, too! Maria clucked her tongue. As a matter of fact, she had done the bathroom a little too well for Maria's comfort. Was Miss Sullivan trying to tell her something? Was she dissatisfied with Maria's work and trying to show her how she expected the job to be done?

And then a terrible thought struck Maria: Had Miss Sullivan actually gone out and hired a new girl to replace her?

No no, Miss Sullivan was a good woman, a fair woman. She would never do so cruel a thing as that. There had to be another explanation. Maria was doing a good job, Miss Sullivan had told her so many times. Could Maria do better? Yes, she supposed she could. One could always do better.

When she started to work for Miss Sullivan sixteen years ago Maria cleaned the whole apartment the way this bathroom was cleaned now. Maybe over the years she had gotten a little less careful. It was only natural to become a little less careful when you did the same job for sixteen years.

Which was not to say that Miss Sullivan hadn't been wonderful to Maria, and given her raises and Christmas bonuses every year. Although, to be perfectly honest about it, the raises and bonuses had not exactly equaled those of her friends who hadn't worked for the same person for sixteen years.

Still, Miss Sullivan deserved Maria's very best effort, and from now on Maria would give her only that.

Maria finished changing into her black uniform with the white collar and exited the bathroom. She went to the service closet and withdrew the vacuum cleaner and the buckets with rags and Comet and Windex and Soft Scrub.

Maria went into the kitchen and saw that the kitchen was as spotless as the rest of the place. Even the bottoms of the copper pans hanging up on the wall were gleaming!

What was going on here anyway? Didn't Miss Sullivan want her to clean today? Where was Miss Sullivan anyway? Probably sleeping late after one of her all-night working sessions.

Maria didn't understand how anybody could work such hours as Miss Sullivan had told her she worked. Maria decided she would just stop by Miss Sullivan's bedroom and see if she was awake, and if she was Maria would ask her if she wanted her to clean today or what.

Maria tapped softly at the bedroom door. There was no answer, but the door was ajar. Maria opened it a little wider and peeked inside. Well, Maria was right. There was Miss Sullivan in bed all right, the covers tucked up under her chin, her eyes closed.

Maria was just about to shut the door and begin cleaning the completely clean apartment when something stopped her. Something on the sheet tucked up under Miss Sullivan's chin. A spot of something dark. Blood? Maybe not blood, but Miss Sullivan was, after all, an old lady, and maybe Maria ought to check.

Maria tapped on the door.

"Miss Sullivan?" she called softly.

There was no response.

"Miss Sullivan?" she said a little louder. "Are you all right, Miss Sullivan?"

There was still no response.

Maybe there *was* something wrong. Maybe, God forbid, Miss Sullivan had had a heart attack! Maria walked tentatively into the room, praying she was wrong, praying everything was all right, praying that Miss Sullivan was just sleeping late because she worked all night and hadn't heard Maria call her name.

Maria reached the bed and discovered that what looked from the doorway like a spot of dried blood on the sheet tucked up over the top of the blankets looked up close *exactly* like dried blood, and now she realized that the blanket under the sheet was soaked with it as well.

"Miss Sullivan!" she screamed, suddenly going cold with panic at not knowing how to give the emergency aid that you were supposed to know how to give to people in situations like this one, and not being able to think of anything better to do, she gave the old lady's cheek a vigorous slap.

The slap must have been harder than she realized. Miss Sullivan's head rolled to the side of the pillow and then Maria saw, to her unspeakable horror, that Miss Sullivan's head was no longer attached to her body but was cut off at the base.

Maria staggered backward, screaming, overwhelmed with dizziness, and vomited onto the bedroom carpet.

CHAPTER 86

RALPH ROBERTS was dumbfounded. What in God's name was Luci Redman doing in his office when she was supposed to be in his East Hampton house, shacking up with Phil Pressman?

"How do you do, Mr. Roberts?" she said. "I am Miss Redman."

Jesus, Ralph thought, she is as dazzling as Phil described her.

"How do you do, Miss Redman?" said Ralph, rising to shake her proferred hand.

"I do hope I'm not intruding, Mr. Roberts, barging in on you like this without any warning."

"No no, not at all, not at all," he said. "May I take your coat?"

"Thank you."

Ralph helped her off with her long black overcoat, then noticed the slash in its left shoulder.

"What happened here?" he said.

She smiled engagingly.

"Somebody attacked me with a meat cleaver," she said.

He laughed, took the coat and hung it up on the back of the door.

"Well, sit down, sit down," he said.

"Thank you," she said.

She took a seat opposite him and crossed her legs. He tried hard not to stare at them.

"So," said Ralph, "how is Phil?"

"Quite well," she said.

"And Julie and the baby?"

"Equally well."

"Good."

An awkward pause.

"So," said Ralph. "What can I do for you today?"

"Well," said Nanny, "I have to ask you for some information."

"Yes?"

"Mr. Pressman gave me the address and telephone number of the place he was going to last night, but in the haste of his departure I fear I've misplaced it."

"I see," said Ralph.

"In point of fact, Mr. Pressman forgot to take the baby's medicine with him, and it's most urgent that I get it to him immediately."

Ralph wrinkled his forehead. He'd been so sure it was Luci

Redman that Pressman was taking out to the house, and *Julie* whom he hadn't wanted to know where he was, that Ralph was having trouble adjusting to the fact that it must have been Julie and the *baby* he'd taken out to the house. If it *had* been Julie and the baby, then maybe the person he didn't want to know his whereabouts was Luci *Redman*.

"What makes you think I know where they went?" said Ralph, stalling for time.

Luci smiled.

"Oh, Mr. Roberts, I *know* you know," she said.

Luci recrossed her legs. It was now possible from a certain angle to see quite a way up her leg. Ralph tried hard not to stare too obviously.

"Listen," said Ralph, "I got to be honest with you. Very frankly, I was told not to say where they went, O.K.? I don't know why, but Phil was very definite about that. So, as much as I'd like to help, I just can't tell you."

"Oh, what a pity," said Nanny, pouting. "How is the baby going to get his medicine?"

"Well, I don't know," said Ralph. "I suppose Phil will realize he's forgotten it at some point, and then he'll either call you or me and we can get it to him."

"Then I take it he's not with you in your apartment?" said Nanny.

"Oh no, of course not," said Ralph.

"But he *is* in the city, is he?" said Nanny.

Ralph sneaked another peek up her dress and when his eyes returned to her face he realized she'd caught him in the act.

"Look," said Ralph, flushing, "I really shouldn't be discussing this with you. I mean he did swear me to secrecy, for one reason or another, and I suppose I ought to respect that."

"Yes, you ought to," said Nanny. "You certainly ought to. You would be disloyal if you did otherwise."

"I'm sorry," said Ralph, standing up and going to get Nanny's coat off the back of the door.

"So am I," said Nanny, allowing Ralph to help her on with her coat.

"Well," said Ralph, "thanks for stopping by."

"Yes," she said, "it was pleasant meeting you."

"You too," he said.

Luci Redman's eyes suddenly widened.

"I'm frightfully sorry, Mr. Roberts," she said, "but I *must* know—where on earth did you get that?"

"Where on earth did I get *what?*" said Ralph, having not the slightest idea what she was talking about.

"That extraordinary belt buckle," she said.

Ralph looked down at his belt.

"This?" he said.

"Yes."

"I've had this for years," he said.

"But it's extraordinary," she said. "My brother had one exactly like it which he bought in the States several years ago and then lost. He was heartsick about it. I'd had it in the back of my mind to get him another if I ever saw one like it, but it completely slipped my mind until this very moment. May I?"

She took a step toward Ralph and touched his belt buckle. Then she slid the tip of the belt back through the loop and unbuckled the belt.

"Yes," she said, "it's exactly like the one my brother lost."

As Ralph watched in mounting disbelief, Nanny pulled the belt out of the loops of his slacks, then clasped the tab of the zipper of his fly and pulled it all the way down.

"What are you doing?" said Ralph in a strange voice.

"Convincing you to tell me where Mr. Pressman went," she said and slipped his pants down over his hips.

Jesus, everything Pressman said about her was true, he thought. Ralph couldn't believe this was actually happening to him.

"I told you," he said quietly, "I can't reveal that information."

"I know you can't," she said, sinking to her knees on the office carpet, "but I suspect you will."

CHAPTER 87

BY THE TIME Detectives Max Segal and Salvatore Caruso rolled up at the San Sebastian Towers it was nearly 10 a.m. and the place was crawling with cops. There were five sector cars with their dome lights flashing, an E.M.S. van and the Crime Scene Unit. The area around the entire building had been sealed off with ropes and signs reading "Crime Scene, Do Not Pass."

Caruso and Segal pushed through the small crowd of curiosity seekers and media people into the lobby, where two uniforms were keeping everyone out.

Caruso, the senior man, flashed his shield at the uniforms.

"Whattaya got?" said Caruso.

"Two D.O.A.'s," said one of the uniforms. "The night doorman and an old lady who lives in the penthouse."

"Where are they?" said Caruso.

"The doorman is down here, the old lady is upstairs," said the younger of the two. "Go upstairs first. It's unreal."

"The M.E. up there yet?" said Segal.

"Nah, he was delayed up in Westchester because of the snow," said the other uniform.

"It's the penthouse, right?" said Caruso.

"Right."

"C'mon, hotshot," said Caruso, leading his partner to the elevator.

Max Segal was one of the youngest cops in the N.Y.P.D. ever to be made detective. He had been routinely looking at stiffs for over a year now. Although he had taken great pains to conceal it from his brutish and battle-scarred partner, Max had never gotten used to looking at dead people.

Looking at dead people no longer bothered most cops, Max knew. Max looked at a dead person and always saw somebody who had been alive a little while ago, just like Max himself, someone who hadn't expected to be lying there dead now.

Max followed Caruso out of the elevator at the penthouse floor and into the old lady's apartment. Two Crime Scene Unit men were busily at work, taking flash photographs of everything in the apartment and dusting every surface for latent prints. Two other plainclothes detectives, Cassidy and Mahoney, were taking notes on everything in sight in little lined spiral notebooks.

Cassidy looked up and saw Segal and Caruso.

"Gentlemen," said Cassidy.

"Whattaya got?" said Caruso, taking out his own little lined spiral notebook, biting off the end of a cigar and sticking it between his teeth.

"Deceased is one Mary Margaret Sullivan, president of the Sullivan, Stouffer, Cohn and McConnell advertising agency," said Cassidy. "The cleaning woman discovered her employer's head lying on the pillow of her bed at approximately 9:08 a.m. Unreal, huh? Go take a look at it, it's really something. The cleaning woman's name is Maria Esposito, incidentally, and she is taking it not at all well."

"Have they interviewed her yet?" said Caruso, fishing in his coat pocket for a book of matches and coming up empty-handed.

"They tried," said Cassidy, "but she appears to be in shock. They've got her in the super's apartment."

"There's no chance she did it then, huh?" said Caruso.

"It's doubtful," said Cassidy. "Maria is fairly petite, and I'd say that quite a lot of strength was necessary to separate that lady's head from her body."

"Where's the rest of the body?" said Segal, not relishing the prospect of having to look at a severed head.

"We don't know yet," said Mahoney. "You want to help us look?"

Max glanced at Mahoney to see if he was serious.

"You're kidding me, right?" said Max. "You really don't know where the rest of the body is?"

"No," said Mahoney, "we haven't located it yet."

"Hey, anybody got a match?" said Caruso.

"Yeah," said Cassidy. "My ass and your face."

"Seriously," said Caruso.

"Seriously?" said Cassidy. "Yeah, I got a pack in my coat pocket in the closet over there. Hey, Max, be a good boy and get Caruso my matches, would you?"

Max walked over to the closet, as Cassidy and Mahoney and the Crime Scene Unit men all stopped to watch. Max opened the door of the closet.

Hanging from a hook on the wall of the closet, its feet resting on the floor, was the headless body of Mary Margaret Sullivan.

CHAPTER 88

NANNY exited the building on Madison Avenue with a smug smile on her face. She glanced at the directions Ralph had scribbled on the sheet of stationery, and then she looked about for a suitable ride.

She stood in the slush of the street at the stoplight and scanned the vehicles waiting for the light to change. She walked past two empty cabs and knocked on the window of a late-model Cadillac Coupe de Ville driven by a stocky, gray-haired man in his midfifties who was wearing a camel overcoat and a blue pin-striped suit.

The man looked at her inquisitively. She motioned for him to roll down his window. He reached over to the passenger side and rolled it down.

"Hello," said Nanny in her most upper-class British accent. "I wonder if I might hitch a ride with you. I'm a nurse and it's an emergency."

"There are two cabs right up there," said the man. "You walked right past them."

"I know," she said, with a beguiling smile. "In point of fact, two young blacks have filched my purse and I'm late for my shift at the hospital. I was wondering if you'd mind awfully dropping me."

The man nodded.

"Hop in," he said.

"Thank you," she said and got in beside him.

The car had red leather upholstery, a Blaupunkt stereo FM radio and tape deck, and a three-hundred-dollar radar detector.

"Lovely automobile," she said.

"Thank you," said the man with evident pride.

"The driver isn't too shabby either," she said.

The man blushed red. The traffic light turned green. The car started forward.

"Which hospital is it?" he said.

"Have you chains on your tires?" said Nanny.

"Of course I have chains on my tires," he said. "Which hospital is it?"

"It's a bit far, actually," she said. "I hope that's all right."

"How far?" said the man.

Nanny giggled.

"Southampton," she said.

"Southampton, England?" said the man, grinning.

"Southampton, Long Island," she said.

"You're kidding me," he said.

"No, as it happens, I'm not," she said.

"Look," he said, stopping the car, "I can't take you to goddam Long Island. I have a job. I have to go to my office."

"Aww," she said, pouting. "Why don't you take a few hours off?"

"Out of the question," he said.

"Will they fire you if you're a few hours late?" she said.

"Oh, they won't fire me," he said. "Don't worry about *that*."

"How can you be so sure?" she said.

"If anyone gets fired in that office, *I'm* the one who'll do the firing," he said.

"Are you that powerful?" she said.

"Yes," he said.

"I find power very interesting," she said.

"Do you?"

"Very interesting," she said. "Very aphrodisiac."

"Is that a fact?" he said, his neck turning scarlet.

"Yes," she said. "What a pity we're both on our way to work."

"A great pity," he said.

They drove awhile in silence.

"I've got an idea," she said.

"What's that?" he said.

"You be late for *your* job and I'll be late for *mine*."

"What?" he said.

"I have a little house in the woods in East Hampton," she said. "We'll go there for a few hours. You can tell me exactly how powerful you are, and then I will make you experience things of an erotic nature that you have never experienced before. Then you can drop me at the hospital."

The man appeared not to have heard what she had said and was silent for three more stoplights. When he finally spoke he looked straight ahead and not at her.

"My wife must never find out about this," he said. "You must give me your absolute honest-to-God word of honor that she will never find out about this."

"Oh, on my honor," she said.

CHAPTER 89

HARRY HAD QUIETED down and Phil put him back on the bed and surrounded him with the cushions. Julie hadn't responded to Phil's entreaties to eat something and he'd temporarily given up. He'd eaten a makeshift baloney sandwich breakfast of his own, standing up over the kitchen sink.

He picked up the telephone and dialed Mary Margaret Sullivan's number. The line rang three times and then a gruff masculine voice answered.

"Crime Scene, O'Malley," said the voice.

"Oh, uh, I'm sorry," said Phil, "I think I must have dialed the wrong number."

"Who'd you want?" said the voice.

"I was dialing the Sullivan residence."

"This *is* the Sullivan residence," said the voice. "Who are you?"

"Oh, I'm Phil Pressman, a friend of Miss Sullivan. Is she there?"

"Miss Sullivan is unable to come to the phone," said the voice. "What is your relation to Miss Sullivan, Mr. Pressman?"

"Who am I talking to?" said Phil.

"This is Lieutenant Patrick O'Malley of the New York Police Department."

"The police department?" said Phil. "Is everything all right? Has something happened to Miss Sullivan?"

"Can you give me the address and phone number of the premises you are calling from, Mr. Pressman?"

CHAPTER 90

THE POLICE refused to tell Phil what had happened to Mary Margaret. They kept wanting to know who he was and where he was calling from. Phil hung up and telephoned Ralph Roberts in a fever. Roberts had already heard the news about Mary Margaret Sullivan and was badly shaken.

"She's gone, Phil," said Roberts in a voice that was suddenly old. "Somebody killed Mary Margaret in her apartment late last night."

Phil was incredulous. He simply could not believe what Roberts was telling him. Mary Margaret, dead? It wasn't possible. He'd just *seen* her. As if just having seen somebody would somehow make her invincible. Phil felt orphaned.

"How did it happen?" said Phil. "Do they know?"

"Not yet," said Roberts.

"Oh God," said Phil, half to himself, "what are we going to do?"

"Well, we'll all miss her, that's for sure," said Roberts, mistaking his meaning. "The agency will, of course, survive without her. Listen, Phil, before I forget—you left the baby's medicine in New York."

"I what?"

"The medicine that the baby takes," said Roberts. "You forgot to bring it with you."

"What medicine are you talking about?" said Phil. "The baby doesn't take any medicine."

"I don't know what medicine it is," said Roberts, "but Luci Redman came up here specially to make sure it got to you, so it must be pretty important."

"Luci Redman came to your *office*?" said Phil.

"Yeah," said Roberts. "She seemed really worried. She wanted to know where you went so she could get this medicine to you."

Phil felt his chest tighten.

"Ralph, please don't tell me you gave her the address here," said Phil, "please don't."

"Well, I wasn't going to," said Roberts, "but she was so insistent. *Extremely* insistent, Phil . . ."

A whisper:

"You *told* her?"

"I got to be honest with you," said Roberts, "I really thought you were out there with Luci, shacking up. I really thought it was your *wife* you didn't want to know."

"You did tell her, then?" said Phil.

"Yeah," said Roberts, "I did. Hey, I sure hope I didn't do the wrong thing, kid . . ."

"How long ago did she leave your office, Ralph?" said Phil, his mind racing, trying to think what to do first.

"Oh, let's see. About three, three and a half hours ago. Not more than that. She should be there any minute now if the roads have been plowed."

"Ralph, I have to go now," said Phil, and abruptly hung up the phone.

Nanny knew where they were! Nanny was coming here! He had to get Julie and Harry out of the house at once!

CHAPTER 91

BY 11 A.M. the detectives had interviewed Maria Esposito the cleaning woman, Enrique Marquez the morning doorman, Hector

Montalban the super and half a dozen of the tenants. Not a single useful fact had emerged from any of the interviews.

The Crime Scene Unit had finished taking photographs and left. The medical examiner finally made it in from Westchester and did a preliminary examination of the bodies and went on to his office at the morgue at Thirtieth Street and First Avenue.

The body of Otto Montag the doorman and the head and the rest of Mary Margaret Sullivan had all been 95-tagged and sent to the morgue to be autopsied. A meat cleaver had been recovered and tagged as a possible murder weapon.

Max had recuperated from the grisly shock of opening the closet door and discovering the headless body, and his colleagues had recuperated from the unalloyed hilarity of Max's reaction.

"So what have we got so far?" said Lieutenant O'Malley.

"If you want my opinion," said Caruso, "it was junkies."

"Yeah," said Cassidy. "I vote for junkies too. The way I see it, they hear that this rich advertising lady is living up here in the penthouse, and maybe they figure she's got lots of jewelry and shit laying around . . ."

"The doorman doesn't give them access," said Mahoney, "so they homicide him. Then they go upstairs to the penthouse. The old lady puts up a struggle and they go apeshit and cut her up."

"That's about the way I figure it too," said Caruso.

"It's about the only scenario that makes any sense," said Cassidy.

CHAPTER 92

THE MAN had been making excellent time. Only one lane had been plowed on the Long Island Expressway and the Sunrise Highway, but so many people had stayed home from work today because of the blizzard that there was very little traffic. Route 27 had been slower going than the expressway, but now they were almost there.

As the Cadillac made the turn off of Sleepy Pond Drive onto Live Oak Road, Nanny could see that they were almost there and she no longer needed him.

"How far down is your driveway, honey?" said the man, scanning the street.

"It's not far," she said, "but I'm afraid I have a confession to make to you."

"What's that?" he said.

"I don't know how you're going to take this," she said, "but I think I had better tell you."

"Go ahead."

"I have herpes," she said.

The man's face darkened.

"You dragged me all the way out on fucking Long Island for three-and-a-half fucking hours to tell me you have fucking *herpes*?" he said angrily.

He stopped the car with a jolt. It skidded a quarter turn to the left.

"I'm sorry," she said. "I knew if I told you before we got here you wouldn't come."

"And why the fuck are you telling me *now*?"

She looked at him sweetly.

"Because, while talking to you on the way out, I decided you're too decent to be lied to," she said. "I'm terribly ashamed. I really did want to make love to you. I hope you'll find it in your heart to forgive me."

She reached for the door handle to get out.

"Wait," he said.

"Yes?"

"You're telling me the truth now?" he said dubiously. "You really liked me too well to lie to me?"

"That's right."

"And you really did want to make love to me?"

"That's right."

He considered this a moment and sighed.

"All right," he said.

"Pardon me?"

"All right, let's do it," he said.

"You mean you don't mind that I have herpes?" she said.

He shrugged.

"I've got condoms in the glove compartment. Besides, I'm about ninety percent sure I've got a dose of it myself," he said, pulling her forward in an embrace.

She submitted to the kiss for several moments, then snaked her hand into her pocket and withdrew the knife she'd gotten from Mary Margaret Sullivan's kitchen.

Lining it up carefully behind his back, she exhaled loudly and plunged the blade through the man's heavy camel coat, through his blue pin-striped suit, through his blue oxford cloth shirt, through his white T-shirt, through the skin of his back and deep into his left lung.

CHAPTER 93

PHIL ran into the bedroom and got Harry, wrapped him in his blanket and carried him out to the Jeep. He unlocked the car, put Harry in the infant seat, locked him into it, slammed the door and raced back to the house.

Things were going too fast for him. Mary Margaret was dead. Nanny was on her way out here to get them. Had Nanny gone to Mary Margaret's apartment as he had feared she would? Was it Nanny who'd killed Mary Margaret? He was unable to think clearly. His thoughts kept running together.

He pulled Julie out of bed, tried to jam her boots onto her feet, and in his panic was unable to do anything. His hands were shaking.

Slow *down*, he told himself, panic will only make you unable to function. Slow down and get a grip on yourself and you might be able to handle this. Keep going the way you are going, and you and your family will all surely die.

He dragged Julie out of the house and through the snow and over to the Jeep and jammed her into the front seat on the passenger's side. He got into the driver's seat, locked all the doors in the car and put the key in the ignition and turned it over. It didn't start.

Oh no, oh please, God, *no*, he prayed. Let it start, please please *please* let it start!

He turned the key again, and started frantically pumping the gas pedal. Nothing. Nothing at all. The engine didn't even turn over.

He unlocked his door, got out and went around to the front of the car and tried to open the hood and couldn't. He knew there had to be a hood release somewhere inside the car and climbed back in again, and under the dashboard on the left he found the handle marked "Hood" and pulled it and heard the hood pop up.

He ran back out to the front of the car, reached under the popped hood and lifted it up. He didn't know very much about cars, but whenever he'd had trouble with cars in the past he'd always looked under the hood and often he'd been able to find something obvious that was wrong and sometimes he'd even gotten it to work.

He looked under the hood. The layout of the parts in the Jeep Cherokee's engine compartment was unfamiliar, but the trouble this time was quite obvious and it didn't take him long to spot it at all: Somebody had taken out the battery.

CHAPTER 94

I MUST CALM DOWN, he thought, as he dragged Harry, who was now screaming his head off, out of the infant seat and out of the car and back into the house and back into the nest in the bed surrounded by cushions. I must not think about the fact that Nanny is already here and has taken the battery out of the car and is waiting to get us, I must keep on doing whatever I can do as long as I am alive to do it, because there is nothing else that I can do right now.

He raced back to the car and dragged Julie out of it and back through the snow and into the house and into the room where she'd spent the night and into her bed, and then he raced back to the door they came in through and locked it and went and found the steak knife and the poker and with one in each hand stood looking out into the forest and tried to breathe slower and calm down.

All right, he thought, I have gotten this far. That is something. She could have struck us when we were outside, when I was carrying Harry or when I was carrying Julie, and I couldn't have done a thing about it then, but she didn't, and now at least I have them both back inside again, and we are safe again, at least temporarily,

Unless.

Unless, he thought, while I was out at the car Nanny crept inside the house and she is in here with us now.

CHAPTER 95

PHIL tiptoed stealthily from room to room, poker in his right hand, steak knife in his left, his heart hammering in his ears. She is in here, he thought, in one of the rooms of this house, right now, waiting for me. But which one?

His pulse in his ears was nearly deafening. His respiration was shallow and so erratic and so loud he had to keep holding his breath to listen for the telltale sounds of the person who was stalking him.

Which rooms had he already checked? Harry's room—yes. Julie's room—yes. No, wait! Both bedrooms had closets and those he'd forgotten to check. She could be lurking in one of the closets, waiting till his guard was down to strike, waiting to crush his head, waiting to dismember Harry, waiting to disembowel Julie!

Stop! He couldn't afford to think like that! He had to calm down. He had to think clearly. He had to have some kind of plan, some kind of structure, some kind of something or he would fall apart completely.

He was now soaked in sweat. His pulse was racing and his chest was so tight he could hardly get the oxygen in and the carbon dioxide out. All right. So he had missed the closets. So he would have to begin all over again.

He crept into Julie's room. He saw nothing. Everything appeared just the same as he had left it. The bed with the covers flung to one side and the pillow which had fallen onto the floor and the . . . Wait, had the pillow been on the floor when he saw this room last? Yes, he remembered now, he'd knocked it onto the floor himself while pulling Julie out of the bed.

He glanced at the closet. The closet door was closed. Had it been closed when he'd left this room a few moments ago? He couldn't remember. The point was, it was closed now. That could mean Nanny was behind the door, waiting to attack. Steak knife and poker at the ready, he crept quietly up to the closet door. He put the knife between his teeth, grabbed the doorknob with his free hand, turned it swiftly and tore open the door.

Nothing. Nanny was not in the bedroom closet. He crept into Harry's room. He advanced stealthily to the closet and flung open the door. Something pitched forward onto his chest and he screamed.

But what had pitched forward against his chest was only the precariously balanced hose and pipe of a vacuum cleaner attachment. He shoved them back in the closet, as Harry, awakened by his scream, started screaming himself.

Phil tiptoed into the kitchen and discovered nothing. The living room. Nothing. The third bedroom. Nothing. The third bedroom closet. Still he found nothing. It now looked as though Nanny must not be in the house after all. It now looked as though she must still be outside, waiting for the right moment to attempt entry.

Trying to watch all eight doors at once was an impossibility. Phil reached for the phone and dialed the operator.

"Operator," said a young male voice.

"Operator," said Phil, his voice breaking in odd places, "this is an emergency. Get me the police."

"Which police would you like," said the male operator, "the Village or the Town?"

"What?" said Phil.

The operator's words did not compute.

"Which police would you like, the Village or the Town?"

"Get me," Phil said carefully, "whichever police you like, but do it *now*."

"Are you in the Village or the Township, sir?" said the operator. "I have to know."

"I don't *know* what I'm in," said Phil. "I just got here. Get me somebody quickly, for God's sake—this is an emergency! My family's lives are in danger!"

"Yes, sir, I'll connect you with the Village Police."

Phil scanned the sliding glass doors. There was no movement outside. Nanny could be anywhere. More than likely, she was in the woods, close to the house. More than likely, she could see him now, could watch whatever he did, could see him right this minute as he talked on the phone, could wait to strike whenever he was most vulnerable.

The line rang four times and was answered.

"Village Police."

"My name is Pressman," said Phil carefully. "My family and I are in great danger. I need you to come out here and get us."

"What is the address there?" said the impassive voice.

"Live Oak Road, off Sleepy Pond Drive," said Phil. "How soon can you be here?"

"Live Oak Road?" said the voice. "That's in the Township, sir, not the Village. You'll have to call the Town Police."

"Didn't you hear what I said? My family is in mortal danger! You're telling me you can't come because I'm not in your goddam *district*?"

"That is correct, sir," said the voice. "I'll put you through to the Town directly."

The connection was broken and then Phil heard a series of clicks and another male voice answered.

"Town Police."

"My name is Pressman," said Phil, his voice again breaking. "My family and I are in great danger. We need you to come out here and evacuate us immediately!"

"What is the danger, sir?"

"Someone is trying to kill us," said Phil. "They followed us out here from the city."

"Who is trying to kill you?" said the voice.

"Someone who works for us," said Phil.

"Like a handyman?" said the voice.

"Actually, it's our nanny," said Phil, aware that this made him sound like a lunatic.

"Why don't you just leave?" said the voice.

"We can't," said Phil, "she stole the battery out of our car."

"She followed you from the city to steal the battery out of your car?" said the voice.

"No no, she . . . Listen," said Phil, "I can't explain it to you now, we just have to get out of here immediately! Will you please come and get us?"

"What is your location, sir?"

"Live Oak Road, off Sleepy Pond Drive! Please hurry!"

"That the Roberts place?"

"Yes!"

"Is Mr. Roberts there with you now?"

"No, he's not here! What is the point of asking if—?"

"Where is Mr. Roberts?"

"In the city! He's in the city! What could it possibly matter where—?"

"Does Mr. Roberts know you're there?"

"Of *course* he knows we're here! He let us have his place to get away from. . . . *Listen*, goddamn it, *are you going to help us or not?*"

"We will, but it won't be for a while, sir," said the voice.

"Why the hell not?"

"We have several emergencies right now that we're trying to handle."

"*Emergencies!*" said Phil. "*This* is an emergency, goddamn you! *Somebody is trying to kill us!* Do you have any emergencies greater than *that?*"

"We'll come as soon as we can, sir," said the voice and the line clicked off.

Phil hung up the phone in frustration and disbelief. The police are supposed to protect us, he thought—how could they refuse to help in an emergency? Maybe they thought he was a nutcase. Maybe he should have mentioned the baby. Why *hadn't* he mentioned the baby? Maybe if he called back and told them that there was a baby involved, they'd come right away.

Phil picked up the phone again and started to dial the operator, and then realized with a sinking feeling in the pit of his gut that the line was dead, that Nanny must have severed it, and now they were completely cut off from the rest of the world.

CHAPTER 96

BY EARLY AFTERNOON Harry sank into a deep slumber and did not come out of it, even when Phil got alarmed and tried to rouse him to feed him his bottle.

It was futile. Like Julie, Harry now appeared to be in some sort of semi-comatose, zombie-like state. If the phone lines hadn't been cut he could have called a pediatrician and asked what to do—not that a pediatrician would have known how to deal with this.

Nanny had caused both Harry's and Julie's comas, of that he was now certain. Goddamn her! She wasn't human. He didn't know what he could do against someone who had such powers. He didn't know what good his steak knife and his poker were going to be against her.

Where the hell was she now and what could she possibly be doing all this time? If she were out in the snow, she'd be freezing, unless creatures like her didn't even feel the cold. Perhaps she was out there chanting and charging up and intensifying the spells she'd put on Julie and Harry, and he was going to be the next one to become a zombie. What the hell was she *waiting* for?

Phil went into the kitchen and searched for things which might have a better chance against Nanny than steak knives or pokers. He looked under the sink and came up with a bottle of Prestone anti-freeze, a red plastic container labeled "Gasoline," several cans of 20W/50 Castrol GTX motor oil, a small propane torch and a baseball bat.

He placed the propane torch and the baseball bat on the counter. He wasn't sure how he might use them against her or why they'd be any more effective than the steak knife or the poker, but the more things he had to choose from the better the chances that one of them might be effective.

He peered into the forest from every door and window, scanning the trees, looking for any signs of movement, but saw nothing. If there were neighbors, their houses weren't visible through the woods. Opening the door and shouting "Help!" would accomplish nothing but broadcast his vulnerability.

Phil was beginning to have a hunch that Nanny wouldn't make her move until nightfall. He fixed himself another baloney sandwich from the groceries he'd bought and ate it, watching the woods. He went to Julie and once more tried to waken her enough to eat, but she couldn't swim to the surface of consciousness long enough to even consider it. He was worried about her not eating, but he had worse problems. He once more tried to wake the baby, but Harry, too, was lost in dreamland.

The sun had oranged and inflated and settled into the horizon, and the blue had returned to the snowbanks.

When it got dark Phil didn't turn on any lamps for fear of making himself an easy target. His eyes had grown accustomed to the gradual disappearance of the light, and with the reflection off the snow it was almost enough to see by.

He continued to scan the line of trees that ringed the house. And then he saw something. A shadow slipping noiselessly through the snow toward the rear of the house. A silence. And then a soft scratching at the back door. He waited, not daring to breathe.

Silence. The sound of the wind. The creaking of an overhead branch, laden with snow. Then another sound, that of a lock being tampered with. And then the most chilling sound of all, that of a door slowly creaking open on its hinges.

This was it, he realized, the moment he'd been waiting for, the showdown. He grabbed the steak knife and stuck it in his belt. He grabbed the propane torch in one hand and the baseball bat in the other and crept stealthily into the kitchen.

Nanny stood just inside the door. Her eyes in the dark were glowing a pale blue color, like the gas jets on a stove.

CHAPTER 97

"GOOD EVENING, Mr. Pressman," said Nanny.

There was something metallic and echoey about her voice now. Jesus, he thought, she really *isn't* human.

"Get out of here," he said.

She took a step forward.

"How have you been?" said Nanny in the eerie voice. "I've been worried about you."

She took another step forward.

"Get out," he said.

"I am ready now to take you and Mrs. Pressman and the baby back to the city," she said.

She took another step forward.

"Get out of here *now*," he said.

She took another step forward.

"I only want to take you and Mrs. Pressman and the baby back to the city," she said. "Why do you tell me to get out?"

She took another step forward. He took a step backward, knowing it was a big mistake.

"I know what you are," he said.

"Do you?" she said.

"I talked to Parsons," he said. "I know what you did to Mary Margaret Sullivan."

"You know nothing," she said, and took another step forward.

"Don't come any closer," said Phil, "I'm warning you."

"Please do not resist what is best for all of us, Mr. Pressman. Please come back to the city with me now. My need to take care of you and your family is very great."

He knew he couldn't take another backward step. He knew he had to stop her now. It was not possible for him to put off the moment of truth any longer.

"Stop right there!" he said. "Don't come a step closer or I'll destroy you!"

"Who thinks he can destroy me?" she said. It was not speaking but hissing.

He took a swing at her with the baseball bat and hit her hard on the left side of her head. The blow threw her temporarily off balance but otherwise did no visible damage.

"I shall see thee dead for this!" She spat at him. "I shall see thee damned to everlasting Hell and rotting in a living grave for this!"

"Go back to Hell or wherever you came from!" Phil shouted. He dropped the bat and lit the propane torch. The flame leapt out with a soft whoosh.

She stepped toward him, reaching out for his throat with both hands.

Holding the softly roaring blowtorch in front of him, Phil advanced on her. She backed up, trying to avoid the flame.

"Get out!" he shouted. "Get out and leave us alone!"

She stood her ground. Phil thrust the torch directly into her face. To his horror, her hair caught fire. She began to shriek in a voice so ghastly it froze the blood in Phil's veins.

Hair aflame, she backed away from him, backed toward the kitchen doorway, backed out of the doorway and into the snow. The flames spread to her clothes and soon she was enveloped in garments of fire, a human torch, screaming and staggering backward into the forest.

She flung herself onto the ground and rolled in the snow, but the flames were not extinguished. She struggled to her feet again and continued staggering backward, still shrieking, retreating into the woods.

Phil stood in the doorway of the house, paralyzed with shock at what he had done, as the illuminated, shrieking being penetrated deeper and deeper into the trees, deeper and deeper, deeper and deeper, until finally he could neither see her flames nor hear her cries.

Phil waited for further indications that Nanny was either dead or alive, but heard nothing. A frigid wind whipped snow off the cedar trees into his face. Shuddering more from the experience than from the cold, Phil went back into the house and locked the door.

There was a very good chance that they had seen the last of Luci Redman. Whatever part of her that was human had to be dead now. But what was not human, he thought, might yet return. The blowtorch had been a formidable weapon against a live Nanny. He couldn't imagine what to use against a dead one.

He went to the cabinet over the sink where earlier he'd seen a bottle of Remy Martin and got it down and pulled the cork and took a mouthful directly from the bottle. The cognac scorched his mouth and his throat as he swallowed it, and he was able to trace its path down his esophagus and into his stomach from the delicious pain.

CHAPTER 98

TONIGHT was the worst night of Phil Pressman's life. He was praying it would not be his last.

It was extremely late in the little house in the snowy woods of eastern Long Island, possibly as late as 3 a.m., but Phil was too frightened to lie down and close his eyes until it got light outside.

The wind was whining through the trees in a particularly unsettling manner. According to the outdoor thermometer, which was swinging back and forth in the wind and knocking against the window as if seeking entrance, the temperature was now hovering slightly above zero.

The snapping logs in the fireplace were maintaining the house at a respectable sixty degrees, but the chill that clung to Phil's body had to do with more than temperature. From the floor-to-ceiling windows in the living room Phil could see the foot or two of snow which had fallen onto the ground in the last couple of days and onto the tall cedar trees which engulfed the house.

Now he thought he heard a noise at the back door, a soft scratching sound like something trying to get in, and felt his chest tighten and his heart pound and suddenly there didn't seem to be enough air in the room for him to breathe. Please don't let what I think is out there be out there, he prayed.

But it was nothing, just a branch scratching against the exterior wall.

He made another check of all the doors in the house and then looked in on the baby. Harry snapped open his eyes and smiled at Phil for the first time in his young life, and Phil's heart melted to see it. It was as if he and Harry were finally able to communicate. It was as if they were finally able to share some marvelous secret joke that he had never understood until now.

Phil picked his baby up and hugged him and kissed him and cuddled with him against his face. Then Phil gave him a bottle. Harry drained the milk voraciously. Phil burped him and put him back down on the bed amidst his nest of cushions. Harry didn't cry.

Phil went in to check on Julie, and she, too, opened her eyes and smiled at him.

"Hi," she said.

"Oh God, it's good to see you alive again," Phil said, and hugged her to his chest.

"Where are we?" said Julie.

"In Ralph Roberts's house in East Hampton," said Phil.

Julie looked confused, as if she'd been delirious, as if she'd awakened from a bad fever.

"What are we doing here?" said Julie.

"We were running away from something, but I think we may have gotten rid of it," said Phil. "We'll know by tomorrow."

"Where's Nanny—is she here?" said Julie.

"God, I hope not," said Phil.

"What?" said Julie.

"Never mind," said Phil. "You wouldn't want to know."

"What?"

"Trust me," he said.

He kissed her and hugged her and tucked her in, and then went into the living room to stand guard over his family for the remainder of the night.

He lay down on the couch in front of the fireplace, and then he got under the covers, being careful to place the blowtorch within easy reach if he should require it.

He fought to keep his eyes open fully ten minutes longer, but the cognac had made him extremely sleepy and soon he felt himself sinking into blackness. A moment later and he was snoring softly.

His sleep was haunted by strange creatures—demons, ghosts, ghouls, banshees, zombies, mummies, vampires, werewolves. Creatures with glowing eyes, creatures with reptilian claws, creatures with long fangs dripping with blood. Creatures in flames and in agony. They advanced on Julie and the baby, and he backed them off with a sword whose handle was fashioned into the likeness of his child.

At the hour of the wolf he ascended through several layers of consciousness to the realization that someone was lying close beside him under the covers of the couch.

Julie! She'd recovered enough to want to join him in bed!

Still at least one level below the surface of wakefulness, Phil grunted happily in his sleep and rolled over to snake his arms about his dozing wife.

But a curious smell pervaded Phil's nostrils. A far from pleasant smell. A charred smell. The smell of ashes. The smell of burnt flesh.

Phil opened his eyes and beheld not Julie, but the burnt body of Nanny lying beside him in the bed.

CHAPTER 99

PHIL bolted from the bed.

The charred body of Nanny—hairless, eyeless, earless, nose-less, ghastly to behold—stirred and sat up, blackened teeth grinning liplessly in her skull. It was the same grotesque smile she'd smiled in the nightmare back in New York when she'd peeled the clothes from her body and the skin from her face.

Phil backed away as the burnt horror on the bed threw off the covers and stood up. Tiny, brittle, blackened pieces of her snapped off and remained in the sheets.

Phil fled toward the kitchen, with the abomination that was once a person shuffling painfully after him on charred stumps. He stubbed his bare foot, stumbled, pitched forward and fell on the floor, and then scrambled up onto his feet again before it could reach him.

The creature kept on coming.

Phil raced into the kitchen, looking wildly around for something with which to defend himself, but blowtorch, steak knife, poker and everything else were nowhere in sight.

On the kitchen counter was the baseball bat. He seized the baseball bat and whirled around to face the charred abomination which pursued him. He saw nothing. It was gone.

He couldn't believe it—one instant it was pursuing him, the next it had vanished. Had it been there at all or was he hallucinating?

Phil crept cautiously back into the living room, holding his breath, holding his baseball bat in front of him. A cold wind whipped across the room. One of the heavy sliding glass doors in the living room had been pulled open—the thing had gone back outside!

Phil sprang for the door, swiftly rolled it shut again and locked it securely. Then he considered: The doors had been locked before.

The thing had come in anyway. Relocking the doors was hardly going to protect them now. His only recourse now was follow it outside and . . . and what—kill it? How could he kill it—it was dead already. But if he didn't go outside and try once more to destroy it, his wife and child were in mortal danger.

Phil hastily donned his down coat. Then he found the propane torch, picked up the baseball bat, unlocked the sliding glass door and stepped through it to the outside.

CHAPTER 100

HER DECEPTION had worked. She saw him lock the sliding glass door behind him and creep out into the woods. She emerged from behind the door of the living room utility closet where she had hidden herself and waited until he was out of sight.

When he'd ignited her with the blowtorch she had first fled outside and rolled in the snow. When she realized that her aged flesh was burning too brightly to extinguish by that means, she quenched the unimaginable pain of burning to death by staggering into the deep woods, lying down and retreating to the part of her mind that she used to influence Mrs. Pressman and the baby from afar, and utilized it to brake her bodily processes to a shuddering stop.

With respiration, circulation and synaptic responses halted, there was no further sensation of pain. She allowed her flesh to fully oxidize. When the flames finally ran out of fuel, they withered and died. What remained was her skeletal structure and something more elemental than even that. Her great love and her resolve.

Her resolve to bring the Pressmans back to New York and care for them in the manner which they required. Which *she* required.

Mr. Pressman was proving to be unsalvageable. If that continued to be true, then, with great sadness, she would soon be obliged to put him out of his misery. But Mrs. Pressman and little Harry, sleeping peacefully in the back bedrooms, would then be completely hers. She turned and stiffly made her way back down the hall to the room where the baby was sleeping, aware that tiny pieces of her were still crumbling off and remaining on the floor.

CHAPTER 101

JULIE shifted to a more comfortable position under the covers, shoved her fist into the pillow beneath her head to give it a better shape and tried not to wake up completely. From the low level of light permeating her closed eyelids she could tell it wasn't quite dawn yet, which meant that there were still a few more hours left for her to sleep.

She needed to sleep, needed it desperately. She was exhausted in a way that she had never been exhausted before. She stretched and let her body sink down into the too-soft mattress. As her thoughts turned fuzzy and she drifted into drowsiness, she heard the baby scream.

She was instantly alert, struggling to free herself from the covers and stand up. The scream was not that of a baby who was wet or cold or hungry or who wanted to be picked up. The scream was a scream of terror.

Julie found herself strangely wobbly on her legs as she stood up and walked as rapidly as she could out of the room and in the direction of Harry's cries. She wondered if Phil had heard the baby, and if he were already in his bedroom.

The door to the room the screams were coming from was closed. She tried the handle and found it locked.

"Phil? Phil, are you in there?"

She pounded the door. Harry's screams continued.

"Phil, for God's sake, open the door!"

After a few moments the door was unlocked. The door swung inward. Julie entered the darkened room.

"Jesus, Phil, what's going *on?*"

It was too dark to see anything. Julie clawed the wall at the side of the door where the light switch ought to be, found it and flipped it on. Her eyes were momentarily dazzled by the bright light, and then she saw it.

The hideous burnt thing stood between her and the bed where Harry was lying. It was the most repulsive thing she had ever seen in her life—a blackened skeleton, with tiny shreds of charred flesh hanging from it. A faint clicking was coming from what might once have been a throat and vocal cords.

The thing reached out for her. She shrieked and staggered backward. The thing appeared to be perplexed by her reaction. She felt dizzy and wondered if she'd faint or vomit. She had to get out of the room. She had to save her baby. She screamed Phil's name as loudly as she could and hurled herself past the thing and toward her baby.

CHAPTER 102

WHEN PHIL heard Julie's screams he instantly realized their cause. He began slogging back toward the house through the deep drifts of snow as fast as he could travel. He reached the sliding glass door from which he'd exited, gave it a vigorous yank and realized he had locked it behind him.

Cursing, he threw the bat into the snow at his feet, stuck the propane torch into the space between the waistband of his pants and his body, and fumbled with Roberts's keys. He tried repeatedly to open the door, but his hands were shaking too severely to fit the key into the lock.

In desperation he picked up the bat and smashed it hard against the thermal pane. The safety glass shattered in slow motion, millions of tiny cracks spiderwebbing outward in all directions, but the surface of the door remained intact. Phil swung his bat again and again until the plastic holding the shattered pieces together gave way and formed a hole big enough for him to step through. Phil entered the house and raced toward the sound of Julie's screams.

At the doorway of Harry's room he stopped. Julie, half standing, half sitting on the bed, was clutching the terrified baby to her chest. Between them and Phil stood what was left of Nanny.

The ghastly thing staggered toward him. He backed several steps into the hallway, then raised the bat and brought it down with all his might on the thing's left shoulder. With a sickening sound, the shoulder shattered, sending brittle brown-black pieces of bone flying in all directions. The arm fell off.

Incredibly, the thing took another step toward him. Phil took another step backward. The one-armed thing followed. They were now well clear of the bedroom door.

"Run, Julie, run!" Phil shouted.

Julie slid off the bed and hurtled through the doorway, shielding Harry as best she could.

"Run outside!" Phil shouted. "Run to the car!"

Julie opened the nearest sliding glass door and fled. Phil swung out savagely with the bat again and missed. The force of his swing and his failure to connect with his target threw him gravely off balance and he toppled to the floor, crashing into the sharp corner of a bookcase, severely cutting his shin, the bat flying out of his hands in the process.

Little starbursts of pain exploded in front of his eyes. Warm liquid ran from his shin, soaking his pantleg. The thing advanced till it was standing directly over him. He pulled the blowtorch out of his pants and lit it. The soft bluish flame whooshed out.

The thing made clicking sounds in the area of its throat, lunged forward and kicked the propane torch out of Phil's hands. The lit torch went skittering across the floor and came to rest on a white shag rug. The shag rug, made of some synthetic fiber which had never known a sheep, burst instantly into flames.

Phil dragged himself painfully toward the bat, as the flames from the rug licked at the couch. The couch, constructed of polyurethane foam, ignited with a roar. Phil clutched the bat with both hands, and, as the thing came for him again, used it to pull himself to a standing position.

Smoke and noxious fumes were pouring out of the burning couch and rug. Phil braced himself against the wall, raised the bat above his head and, with an audible exhalation of rage, brought it down with all his might on the thing's skull. The skull imploded at the impact, and Phil heard an otherworldly shriek of agony echo through the burning house.

In a demonic fury, Phil swung the bat wildly as the flames crackled all around him, again and again and again and again, scoring glancing blows and complete misses and direct hits, until the effigy that once was Nanny had been chopped down and blasted into chunks and fragments of black bone and rubble, and still he hammered and pounded away at it until the rubble was gravel on the floor and then it was over, it was finally over, it was completely over, and Nanny was no more.

The fire had curtained the walls and was now eating up the ceiling. Sobbing with exhaustion and relief, soaked in sweat and his own blood, gagging from the smoke and noxious fumes of burning polyurethane, Phil dragged himself out through the hole he had chopped in the sliding glass door and out of the wildly burning building to the cold sweet air outside.

CHAPTER 103

ON THE 14TH OF FEBRUARY, Valentine's Day, Phil Pressman, released from the three-year lease on the apartment he'd rented in the heart of the wholesale meat district on the Lower West Side of Manhattan, watched the last of the Pressman family's belongings being loaded onto the huge moving van which would transport them to their new home.

Then he packed his wife and son into a cab for the final trip to LaGuardia Airport and the flight back to Chicago.

Phil had gotten his old job back at the agency on Michigan Avenue, and Julie was eager to go back to the decorating business at the Merchandise Mart.

Phil and Julie did not blame New York for all that they had gone through, but they'd decided that they really preferred Chicago, arctic winters notwithstanding.

Nanny's jewelry had proven to be even more valuable than Phil dreamed—he'd sold it for a staggering two hundred thousand dollars. Although it had not really been his to sell, Phil figured they were entitled to the money—Nanny had caused them at least two hundred thousand dollars worth of grief. Since Ralph Roberts's insurance covered little of what he'd lost in the fire, Phil split Nanny's jewelry money with his former boss.

Together with Phil's salary at the agency and the income that Julie managed to bring in from decorating, the remaining half of the money would be enough to live on for quite some time, enough to move into a house big enough to contain Harry and as many more brothers and sisters as Phil and Julie were able to manufacture—now that Harry was definitely over the colic, other siblings were a distinct possibility.

But no matter how prosperous they might become, there was one thing upon which Phil and Julie were firmly agreed—they were definitely going to raise their family without a nanny.

CHAPTER 104

IT WAS almost closing time at the Sterling Personnel Agency in Santa Barbara, California, and as the sunlight slanted across the newly polyurethaned, knotty pine floor of her office, Clara Winston was just concluding her interview with the new job applicant.

Quite frankly, Clara was impressed.

The slim blonde woman in front of her with the fresh rosy cheeks, the petite figure and the delightful Southern accent was energetic, vivacious, polite, and had a surprising amount of experience for one so young. She was also one of the most astonishingly beautiful women that Clara had ever met.

Indeed, if this young woman weren't so obviously good at what she did and had she not so obviously loved her profession, Clara felt sure she could be a movie star.

Not that physical beauty had ever been a quality actively sought in nannies, thought Clara, but nobody who saw this young woman could possibly fail to fall in love with her.

"Well," said Clara, "I am delighted you got in touch with us, and I feel certain we will be able to place you with an excellent family in Santa Barbara in no time at all."

"Thank you, Clara Winston," said the pretty blonde woman, "it was a real pleasure meetin' you."

"And," said Clara, smiling, "it was a real pleasure meeting *you*, Luci Redman."